Dear Reader,

I love linking characters, getting to really know them and following their development through different stories and situations.

I first met Xavian at the end of the Karedes miniseries. I could vividly picture him and really wanted to write his story, so I was thrilled when I was asked to write the opening book for the Dark-Hearted Desert Men quartet.

At first I couldn't imagine being in Xavian's situation—a charismatic, powerful king who has everything, and I mean everything, taken from him. In fact the more I explored his situation the more I understood how dire it must feel for him. Xavian was probably entitled to a little "woe is me" and if I was nice I would have given him a supremely understanding heroine. But I'm not that nice and, anyway, that would have been too easy. Layla is complex and sexy and powerful in her own right and I loved getting to know her and watching the sparks fly between them—actually, their relationship sizzles so much that I suggest you get a fan.

They really were two wonderful characters to write and I was more than a little sad to say goodbye—however, there are three sexy cousins still to come in this series, all with fantastic stories of their own, so I'm cheered to know that I don't have to say farewell to the Kingdom of Qusay just yet.

Happy reading,

*Carol Marinelli* x

Many years ago there were two Mediterranean islands ruled as one kingdom—Adamas. But bitter family feuds ripped the kingdom apart and the islands were ruled separately. The Greek Karedes family reigned supreme over glamorous Aristo and the smoldering Al'Farisi sheikhs ruled the desert lands of Calista!

When the Aristan king died, an illegitimate daughter was discovered—Stephania, the rightful heir to the throne! Ruthlessly, the Calistan sheikh Zakari seduced her into marriage to claim absolute power but was overawed by her purity and succumbed to love. The kingdom is now ruled in the spirit of hope and prosperity.

But a black mark hangs over the Calistan royal family still. As young boys three of King Zakari's brothers were kidnapped for ransom by pirates. Two safely returned, but the youngest was swept out to sea and never found and presumed dead. But then at Zakari and Stephania's wedding a stranger appeared in their midst. The ruler of a nearby kingdom—Qusay. A stranger with scars on his wrists from the pirates' ropes. A stranger who knows nothing of his past—only his future as a king!

What will happen when Xavian, King of Qusay discovers that he's living the wrong life? And who will claim the Qusay throne if the truth is unveiled?

**Find out in the brand-new Presents® miniseries**

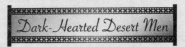

One kingdom. One crown. Four smoldering desert princes. Which one will claim the throne and who will they claim as their brides?

Book 1: *Wedlocked: Banished Sheikh, Untouched Queen* by Carol Marinelli
Book 2: *Tamed: The Barbarian King* by Jennie Lucas
Book 3: *Forbidden: The Sheikh's Virgin* by Trish Morey
Book 4: *Scandal: His Majesty's Love-Child* by Annie West

# Carol Marinelli

## WEDLOCKED: BANISHED SHEIKH, UNTOUCHED QUEEN

*Dark-Hearted Desert Men*

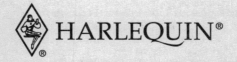

# HARLEQUIN®

TORONTO • NEW YORK • LONDON
AMSTERDAM • PARIS • SYDNEY • HAMBURG
STOCKHOLM • ATHENS • TOKYO • MILAN • MADRID
PRAGUE • WARSAW • BUDAPEST • AUCKLAND

Recycling programs
for this product may
not exist in your area.

ISBN-13: 978-0-373-23672-5

WEDLOCKED: BANISHED SHEIKH, UNTOUCHED QUEEN

First North American Publication 2010.

Copyright © 2010 by Harlequin Books S.A.

*Special thanks and acknowledgment are given to Carol Marinelli for her contribution to the Dark-Hearted Desert Men series*

www.eHarlequin.com

**Printed in U.S.A.**

## All about the author...
### *Carol Marinelli*

**CAROL MARINELLI** finds writing a bio rather like writing her New Year's Resolutions. Oh, she'd love to say that since she wrote the last one, she now goes to the gym regularly and doesn't stop for coffee and cake and a gossip afterward; that she's incredibly organized and writes for a few productive hours a day after tidying her immaculate house and taking a brisk walk with the dog.

The reality is Carol spends an inordinate amount of time daydreaming about dark, brooding men and exotic places (research), which doesn't leave too much time for the gym, housework or anything that comes in between. And her most productive writing hours happen to be in the middle of the night, which leaves her in a constant state of bewildered exhaustion.

Originally from England, Carol now lives in Melbourne, Australia. She adores going back to the U.K. for a visit—actually, she adores going anywhere for a visit—and constantly (expensively) strives to overcome her fear of flying. She has three gorgeous children who are growing up so fast (too fast—they've just worked out that she lies about her age!) and keep her busy with a never-ending round of homework, sports and friends coming over.

A nurse and a writer, Carol writes for the Harlequin Presents® and Medical Romance lines and is passionate about both. She loves the fast-paced, busy setting of a modern hospital, but every now and then admits it's bliss to escape to the glamorous, alluring world of her heroes and heroines in Harlequin Presents novels. A bit like her real life actually!

# PROLOGUE

LAYLA did not close her eyes as the hand-maidens veiled her. Instead, she watched in the mirror as, one by one, her generous cleavage, her pale legs and the delicate henna tattoos disappeared beneath the golden layers of the jewelled gold dress. Then she stared as her long raven hair and her made-up face, her rouged cheeks and full lips also disappeared—till all that was left were her eyes.

Eyes that blinked nervously as the realisation hit—when these veils were removed, this time there would be none of the usual relief. It would not mean she was home at her palace in Haydar, where she could relax. No, when these veils were removed it would be before her new husband—she would be in the Qusay Desert, on her wedding night.

King Xavian Al'Ramiz, the man she had

been betrothed to since her childhood, had after all these years decided to honour that commitment and finally summoned her to be his bride.

He had kept her waiting—and, more importantly for Layla, he had kept her country waiting.

Her life had been—*was*—but a holding pattern.

Layla was the eldest of seven girls. Her mother had died trying to produce a male heir—Layla had heard the sobs and anger as each gruelling birth yielded yet another poor crop—and the deeply traditional Haydar people had, with each birth, further balked at the idea of being ruled by a queen.

Ah, but her father had been wise. A deal had been brokered many years ago with the King of Qusay, whose marriage had produced only one son, that the two would marry. Xavian would step in and appease the people of Haydar, and of course they would produce a son—who would one day rule both lands.

Since the union had not been forthcoming, on her father's death Layla had become Queen. The elders had wanted her to rule in name only, so that they could advise her and keep the ways of the people safe, but she'd intended to take her role seriously. She had asserted herself—refusing to sign or add voice to anything that she didn't agree with.

And as for her early betrothal—why, Xavian had been too busy being a bachelor to give up his ways. It had taken his parents' death to force his hand—and she had grown up a lot while waiting for his summons to marry. Layla had ruled her land her way, and responsibility had made her wise. Xavian had left it too late to demand compliance, for she would not lie down now and meekly hand it all over to a man who had no real interest in either her kingdom or in her as a wife.

His parents' recent death had clearly prompted an urgent reappraisal, and the playboy Prince had returned from Europe and stepped magnificently into the role of King of Qusay. A born leader, despite his private loss, he was leading his people through grief-stricken times—Layla knew, because Layla had watched. They had never once spoken, she had seen him only from a distance and merely heard about his decadent ways, but more recently she had made time in her busy schedule to follow him more closely—recording and watching his speeches, which were eloquent and commanding. He was Prince Xavian no more, but a true king.

And a king needed a bride.

It was a business deal.

Layla was aware of that, and yet as she had watched him from afar, watched the man who would one day be her husband live his wild, debauched ways, she had been jealous rather than angry. Jealous that it was all right for Xavian to take lovers, to live wild and free, while she waited.

She was twenty-six.

And tonight, finally, it was her turn.

Tonight, whether or not it was a business arrangement, a convenient betrothal, even if they would for the most part spend their lives apart, tonight he would take her to the Qusay Desert.

Tonight Layla would face her husband… She was suddenly glad of the veils, because beneath them she blushed… Tonight King Xavian Al'Ramiz would become her lover.

Her only lover.

Bizarrely, she wished that he were just a little less good-looking, that the face she had tracked in newspapers, on television and on the Internet did not have such brooding, haughty appeal. How she had scrutinised his features—pausing the footage at times and catching her breath as his black eyes stared back at her. He *looked* royal—from the straight Roman nose to the razored cheekbones, to the lush, thick black hair that fell into perfect shape. He *was* from good lineage.

He had an aura too—a natural confidence, a presence that surrounded him. She herself had witnessed it, unseen from a distance, when their schedules had had them attending the same functions. Layla, hidden behind a veil, had watched her husband-to-be, hoping those black eyes might seek her out, that he might give her a smile or even a brief acknowledgment—*anything* that might indicate curiosity towards his future wife.

He had given her nothing.

Less than nothing. He had stood beside her at the Coronation of Queen Stefania of Aristo last year and quite simply ignored her.

The shame of that day still burnt—his disregard, his obvious boredom at their forthcoming union still humiliated Layla even now.

'Your Highness…' She screwed her eyes closed in impatience as, now that she was veiled, Imran, one of her many advisors, came into her room to deliver some last-minute concerns, to detail some points, to request final instructions in his nasal voice, before his Queen took a rare week off from official duties.

'And we need an urgent signature on the amended sapphire mine proposal…'

*It was her wedding day*!

But duty had to come first, and as Queen of Haydar there was much duty. An entourage had come with her to Qusay for the wedding: a team of advisors, along with handmaidens and her chief lady-in-waiting, Baja.

Oh, how the advisors and elders rued the day the Queen had first voiced her opinion, had refused to just say yes and let them continue on with the ways of old. Instead, to their displeasure, Layla continued to assert herself—which meant reminding them constantly that, as Queen, all decisions were ultimately hers…

It was wearying, exhausting in fact, to be constantly checking and double-checking facts and figures, knowing that her so-called team were permanently on the alert for weakness, for that moment when they could slip a document past her unnoticed, when her eyes might miss a small sub-clause… They wished that Haydar might remain staid and unchanged, instead of embracing the many opportunities the rich land offered her people.

'All of this can wait!' Layla fixed Imran with a stare. 'I will sign nothing today.' She watched his lips tighten. 'It can all wait for my return.'

'The drilling is due to commence…'

'It will commence on my return!' Layla snapped. 'When I have read the amendment and if I then approve it.' Yet, despite her strong words, she could feel tears sting her carefully kholled eyes—tears she would never let Imran see, so she turned to the window and stared out to the Qusay ocean.

*It was her wedding day*!

Surely, *surely*, she had earned the right to be nothing but a woman for one day and one night?

Seemingly not!

'We also need to discuss extending the King's visit to Haydar…' Imran was relentless.

'There can be no discussion, till we are married,' Layla responded with her back still to him, knowing that if he saw weakness Imran would pounce. 'Now, if you will kindly let me get on with the small matter of my wedding, I can soon turn my full attention back to Haydar.' He was dismissed, but still stood there, and Layla knew what was coming. Over her shoulder she spoke first. 'Let me just reiterate: nothing, and I mean *nothing,* is to be approved in my absence.'

'Of course,' Imran replied smoothly. 'Though naturally, if it were pressing, you would trust your Committee of Elders…'

'Imran.' Her tears had dried, and her eyes were steady when she turned and faced him. Her voice, like her orders, was crystal-clear. 'I am taking my computer with me, and if for some reason I cannot be contacted by that medium, you will get in a helicopter and visit me in the desert.'

'I would have thought you would prefer not to be disturbed,' Imran attempted.

'I have told you before, Imran—never presume to know my thoughts.'

'Of course, Your Highness.'

He left then, and, even though it was but a

moment from her wedding, the knot of tension in her stomach was reserved for Imran.

'Breathe, Layla,' Baja said gently.

Baja, dear Baja, who stayed silent in meetings but heard everything. Baja, who saw the tears she cried some nights. Baja, the only person who truly understood the daily weight on her shoulders.

'He will use the time I am away to do something...' Layla said.

'He would be a fool,' Baja said. 'Your orders were clear.'

'They twist my words.'

'Then write them down.'

She was so grateful for Baja, for her wisdom, her patience, and *almost* absolutely Layla trusted her.

Almost—because Layla had long ago learnt that the only person she could truly trust was herself.

'I will.'

'First, though,' Baja said, 'you are to marry.'

She was led through the Qusay palace, its corridors lined with ancestral portraits. It was easier to think of a painting on a wall, to focus on the wide doors that were being opened or listen to the swish of her veil as she walked, than to attempt to comprehend that in just a moment she would be beside him.

The desert heat hit her as soon as she stepped outside. She was led down a white path and through manicured gardens—a true desert oasis. Tiny birds like jewels coloured the trees, their wings flapping as rapidly as Layla's eyelashes as finally she stood and waited for her groom.

The marriage service would be small— next week when, as was Haydar tradition, she was unveiled as a married woman, they would be presented to dignitaries and rulers at a formal reception, but for today it was only the judge and senior elders from both lands that would bear witness.

She stood in the relatively cool shade of an orange tree, smelt the fragrant blooms of the gardens, listened to the continual trickle of the fountains, and still she waited.

He had kept her waiting ten years, so what did ten minutes more matter? Layla asked herself.

Or another ten!

A chair was brought for her, but Layla refused. Instead she stood, burning in shame—could this man make it any clearer how little regard he had for her?

She wanted to walk.

She wanted to turn her back on tradition, to demand transport, to tell him where he could shove his business arrangement.

'The King will be here shortly.'

She stared down at her hands, saw her fingers tightly knotted, had to physically plant her feet to the ground to stop herself turning and walking—had to purse her lips behind the veil to prevent herself from saying something that her people would surely regret if she did.

'Perhaps Your Highness should sit…' Again the chair was suggested. One of the ancient judges was already sitting and fanning himself. Perhaps they would bring out refreshments, Layla thought wildly, or cut up the oranges from the heavily fruited trees. And then they could all stand around sucking their quarters as they discussed what to do when a King refused to appear for his own wedding.

This was the hell of duty.

To stand.

To be shamed.

To wait.

* * *

Layla would take it for her people—would go ahead with this union if that was what tradition dictated—but she swore to herself as she stood there, pale and close to fainting, yet still refusing to sit, that he would pay for his offensive behaviour.

If he thought he could treat her so poorly, if he thought she would meekly comply, would trot along by his side and follow his orders, then that was his misfortune.

King Xavian should have done his research more thoroughly. Should have known that behind these veils was a strong, proud woman.

That behind the throng of elders and aides was a ruler who was strong—too strong, according to them.

Tonight she would tell him in no uncertain terms what she thought of his behaviour. He had no idea what awaited him, Layla thought, a small smile of satisfaction spreading over her lips. But it soon faded…

As still he made her wait.

# CHAPTER ONE

KING XAVIAN AL'RAMIZ read the letter again.

It was one of many wishing him well for his wedding day.

It was from King Zakari of Calista, extending his congratulations and saying that he was looking forward to greeting him formally next week at the official reception.

It was the third letter.

The first had offered condolences on the death of his parents and invited him to stay as a guest at the Calistan palace.

Xavian had not responded. That letter he had burnt.

Then another had arrived, to thank him for the Qusay people's gift on the birth of their son, Prince Zafir.

Still Xavian had not replied, though he had kept the letter for a few days, taking it out and reading it over and over till finally it had been tossed into a fire.

And now this.

There was nothing untoward about it, Xavian told himself as he read the letter for perhaps the hundredth time. He did not know what he sought from the words. There were hundreds such letters, offering good wishes, yet Xavian couldn't help himself reading between the lines of this one…

His bride was waiting for him, he was already unforgivably late, yet still he pondered over the page.

It was a formal letter from King Zakari of Calista and his wife Queen Stefania of Aristo. Their union had reunited the Kingdom of Adamas. So why, Xavian pondered, had Zakari, instead of using the Adamas crest, chosen instead to write on Calistan paper? Xavian stared at the coat of arms, ran a finger over the crest, and could not fathom why it troubled him, it just did.

He had been troubled since Queen Stefania's coronation, since she had looked into his eyes and he had registered shock…

No, Xavian told himself, not shock. She had been close to fainting, and he had spoken to her till her husband had realised there was a problem and gently led her away. She had been pregnant, as it turned out, which explained everything.

Except it didn't.

Because the trouble in his soul had started before Stefania had greeted him—as King Zakari had made his way down the line. The rapid beat in his heart had started…a rapid beat that woke him at night, that was here again at this very moment.

Though he could not quite accept it as such, it was fear.

'All is ready, Your Highness.' Xavian didn't turn his head as Akmal, his vizier, came into his suite. 'Your bride awaits.' He could hear the slightly uneasy note in Akmal's voice—after all, his bride, Queen Layla of Haydar, had been waiting for a while now, the proceedings were ready to commence, and yet the groom so far had not made an appearance. Akmal had come yet again to the royal chamber himself, to ensure nothing untoward had occurred, only to find the groom where he had left him last time—still standing at the French windows, still holding the letter and staring broodingly out to the ocean.

'I will be there shortly.'

'Your Highness, may I suggest…?'

'Did you hear what I said?' Only then did Xavian turn, his black eyes furious at the intrusion, shooting the aide down and reminding him who was King. Dressed in the full military uniform of Qusay—superb olive cloth, his chest decorated with medals, his legs encased in long black leather boots, a sword at his side and golden thread holding on his *kafeya*—Xavian cut an imposing figure. But then, Xavian always did—standing six feet two, with broad shoulders and a strong, muscular frame, he did not need medals or swords or royal gold braid to command respect.

'She can wait till I am ready.'

'Your Highness.' Akmal knew better than to argue, so instead he gave a small bow and left. Alone again, Xavian carried on gazing out to the ocean.

She *would* wait. Xavian knew that.

She had already waited a decade for this day. Betrothed to her since childhood, he should have married her ten years ago, but he had chosen not to—he had concentrated on enjoying his freedom instead.

Only now it was over.

Xavian walked out onto the balcony and wished that it gazed to the desert, not the ocean. To the desert, where he found rare peace, to the desert, where he would take his bride tonight.

How weary he was at that thought.

Since his parents had been killed in a plane crash, his advisors had been working overtime. His playboy ways were to end—he was King now, and kings did not live as princes. Kings married and produced heirs, and it was time for Xavian to do the same. After three months of deep mourning, the wedding that he had been putting off must now occur.

It would be a subdued affair, given the circumstances—huge celebrations deemed inappropriate so soon after the country's loss. The people would be informed tomorrow that the King had married, and he would retreat with his bride to the desert before the official reception. After another suitable period of mourning the coronation would take place, and then the people would celebrate. A double celebration, perhaps? The elders had been light on discretion: nine months from the wedding, it would be nice to have a prince on the way.

Xavian had been advised by Akmal to refrain from sexual encounters for a week prior to the wedding—to ensure his seed was plentiful and potent. It was advice Xavian had absolutely chosen to ignore.

Always it was plentiful!

This was a business arrangement and no more. Haydar was struggling under a woman's rule, and Xavian's strong, albeit occasional presence would help guide the troubled country.

Of course he would take a mistress—several, perhaps.

He had no intention of sleeping alone at night.

The unease Xavian felt now wasn't down to wedding nerves, and it wasn't pride that made him deny that he was uneasy. Long before the wedding had been announced, long before his parents had been killed, there had been a deep unrest in his soul.

Trouble he could not define.

A place within that he didn't want to visit.

Sometimes as he stood and stared at a letter, as he did now, searching for clues that surely didn't exist, he actually though he was going mad.

Sometimes at night he would wake with his heart racing. He would feel the beauty in the bed beside him, feel her coil around him, yet he would shrug her off, get up and dress himself, or send her to the mistress chambers. It was not how he wanted to be seen. His heart was racing now, his breath tight in his chest as his black eyes studied the rolling ocean. He felt nausea rising as if he were out there. He could feel sweat beading on his forehead, could feel his body rolling with the waves. The thick scars on his wrists burnt and itched, as they did at times. His eyes scanned the vast ocean, searching for what he didn't know, and then he dragged his gaze away, willed his heart to slow down, for the madness to stop. He comforted himself not with the thought of a virgin bride, but with the solace of the beckoning desert.

Yes!

He would get the wedding over with, take her to the desert, consummate the marriage and then tomorrow he could wander— tomorrow he could take guidance from the heart of the land he now ruled and ask it to bring him peace.

Happier now, he walked from the balcony and through his chamber, the letter still in his hand. He paused at a thick pillar candle and stood watching the heavy cream paper curl and the Calistan crest flare as the flames licked around it. Then he tossed it into the ancient fireplace—just as he had done with the other letters—and with that ritual over he headed to his wedding.

As he opened the door Akmal practically fell inside. Xavian paused for long enough to give his vizier a withering look, and then strode confidently through the palace, past the paintings of his ancestors, down the long corridor and out to the gardens, ready now to get on with his duty.

The elders were seated, but stood when he entered,

His bride did not look round. She stood in a shimmering gold robe, her head veiled, and kept her eyes down as Xavian approached.

He was not looking forward to this!

Haydar was rigid in its ways. The women were covered and robed till they were wed. But even the generous layers of fabric could not disguise her rather rotund shape.

Joy and double joy, thought Xavian wryly. A fat, inexperienced lover to impregnate. Was there no end to his duties?

In a rare concession to modern times the Haydar elders had agreed the announcement would be accompanied by photos—this was not a time for grand feasting and celebration, but it was still much needed good news for the people of Haydar and Qusay.

The judge spoke, asking Layla if she would be a loyal wife, if she would serve her husband, provide him with children, nurture him and their offspring.

Her voice was soft when she agreed.

Again the judge asked her.

Again she said yes.

For the third time it was repeated, and Xavian watched her eyes blink, though still she did not look up at him—as was right.

'I will.'

And then it was Xavian's turn.

Would he provide for her?

It was all that was asked, and only asked once.

A King did not have to repeat himself.

'Yes.'

She glanced up, and the eyes that met his were a deep violet, then long black lashes swept down again. Xavian found himself slightly appeased—they were clear and bright and really rather pretty—perhaps he could ask her to keep them open tonight!

It was over in moments. Their eyes had met for less than a second, yet that was the image that had been captured and would be beamed around the world in the morning. Sheikh King Xavian Al'Ramiz of Qusay and now of Haydar, and his bride Sheikha Queen Layla Al'Ramiz of Haydar and now Qusay.

The long-awaited union was now official.

'We will leave for the desert in an hour…' For the first time he addressed his wife. 'I trust my staff are being helpful?'

She didn't answer. Her eyes still downcast, she gave only a brief nod.

'Is there anything you need?' He attempted conversation, at least tried to put her at ease, but all he got for his efforts was either a nod or a shake of her head. She was refusing to give him even a glimpse of those pretty violet eyes, and Xavian gave a hiss of irritation.

'I will see you in an hour.'

Clearly, Xavian thought, stamping up to his suite, the clip of his boots ringing out on the polished marble floor, it was going to be an extremely uneventful night.

# CHAPTER TWO

'I AM not spending a month there!' Xavian frowned at Akmal as his dresser helped him out of his military uniform and into desert robes in preparation for his honeymoon. 'I agreed only to a week in Haydar.'

'I understand that, Sire, but our advisors are merely responding to what they have heard from the people…' He gave a slightly uncomfortable swallow. 'The Queen was checking the press release and asked that—'

'What?' Xavian's head spun round. He had been admiring himself in the mirror, but Akmal's words demanded curt response. 'Why would you worry her with such details?'

'She asked to see it.' Akmal's lips pursed tightly, so tightly it took a moment for him to release them enough to continue speaking. 'She has also asked that you stay for a month in her land… She feels that the people of Haydar will want to see their new King in residence for a while, so they can fully grasp that you are there for them too. They need this union, Sire…'

Xavian was less than impressed. A week in the desert—that he accepted was necessary. A week: with his new bride at nights, and wandering in his desert by day. After the reception, to appease the people, he had agreed to spend a week in Haydar—where he would formally greet his new people, sign essential documents, and then, apart from necessary formal appearances and the occasional night together at her fertile times, they could get on with their own jobs.

There was unrest in Haydar, though. Xavian knew that. The meek, silent woman he had just married would hardly command respect from her aides, let alone her people. But Xavian was tough. At times there was immense pressure from his elders, from Akmal—just a complete resistance to change—but Xavian was a strong ruler, assured in his role. He never doubted, never questioned that he was right. Yes, he listened to his advisers, he pondered, sought counsel from the desert at times, but always he made *his* decisions—and once they were made he would not be swayed.

No one would dare try.

It must, though, Xavian decided with a smirk, be hell being Queen!

'Two weeks…' Xavian made a rare compromise, but Akmal's brow knitted into a worried frown, for he had already spoken with the Queen. 'Tell her I am prepared to stay in her country for two weeks…'

'I think that a month in Haydar would be wiser…' A soft voice filled the room, and the dresser and Akmal stood aghast as Layla walked, uninvited and unannounced, into the King's chambers!

'You cannot be here…' Akmal was across the room in a flash, ready to scurry her out, but violet eyes halted him. That voice not so soft when she spoke next. 'You will address me as Your Highness…' Still veiled, she stood very still as Akmal bowed deeply. The poor man was clearly torn between royal protocol and protecting his master—only Xavian wasn't annoyed, in fact he was thoroughly enjoying himself, a rare smile dusting his lips as Akmal struggled to appease them both. 'Your Highness, I was about to come to you, to inform you of the King's decision.'

'How tiresome…' She was no longer looking at Akmal. Instead her eyes held Xavian's and the smile slid from his face. 'That a husband and wife must speak through advisors.' Still she held Xavian's eyes. 'Could you inform the King that regretfully, on this detail, the Queen cannot compromise—the people of Haydar need to see that their new King relishes his role, that he wants to help lead them, and a brief visit isn't going to appease them.'

'Your Highness…' Akmal duly started to relay her words. 'The Queen has—'

'Silence!' Xavian snapped to his vizier. 'Leave us.' As Akmal shooed out the dresser he walked slowly to where she stood, but she didn't move, barely blinked. Only her eyes were visible, and this time they did not lower as he approached.

'I have considered your *request*.' Xavian's voice was ominously calm. 'And, as I take my new duties seriously—'

'So seriously,' she interrupted, 'that you could not even be bothered to turn up to your wedding on time!'

How dared she?

She should not question him, should not even let on that she had noticed. Instead she should be proud—proud that the King of Qusay was now her husband—yet he was being greeted with complaints and demands.

'I had my reasons for being late.' He did not need to offer even that, and he *certainly* did not have to tell her his reasons, so why was there still silence?

He had never had to offer an explanation—his decisions, his word, his presence always sufficed. Did she really think he was going to stand there and discuss *reasons*?

She *was* waiting for an explanation.

A mirthless smile spread over his face at her barefaced cheek. Maybe he should tell her, watch her reaction when she found out that her new husband sometimes thought he was going insane—that at times the scars on his wrist burnt so fiercely he thought his skin might rip open, that at times, when sitting quietly, sometimes he could swear he heard a child laughing? He could just imagine her appalled reaction—especially when he told her that he thought that the child was *him*!

'You left me waiting for close to an hour.'

Her eyes never left his. 'And you offer me no explanation—yet you expect me to accept that you take your duties seriously. Today was a duty!' Layla lips were tight beneath her veil. 'And you carried it out dreadfully.'

'Silence!'

His hand splayed as he considered slapping her.

In that instant Xavian, who had never struck a woman—would never strike a woman—considered slapping her. Yet in rapid self-assessment he realised the anger that rose within was in fact directed at himself.

He *had* carried out his duties badly today. Always meticulous, always thorough, he had, on this rare occasion, been tardy. Rarely did he concede, but to be a good ruler sometimes it was necessary. And so, rather than slap her, he did something rare.

'It was not about you.' He saw two vertical frown lines appear between those probing eyes. 'It was not about keeping you waiting, or shirking my duty, or making a mockery of the marriage…' Xavian could hear the words coming from his mouth, yet he could scarcely believe they were his, that for the first time he was explaining himself.

Some of himself.

'A letter arrived…' He saw those lines deepen. 'I should have left it for later. I knew it might well distract me.' He swallowed before continuing. 'And it did.'

He had offered little explanation, but she knew it was more than he had ever given before, and after just a brief moment of hesitation she gave a courteous nod.

'I am sure you have a lot on your mind,' she conceded. 'I, too, missed my parents today, but your loss is more recent. I accept your apology.'

He hadn't actually apologised, Xavian wanted to point out—or had he? Did sorry actually have to be said for it to count as an apology?

Xavian continued. 'If it will please the people to have more time with their new King then I will grant you your month. Of course the people of Qusay will also want time with their new Queen. I suggest that after the desert, instead of heading straight to Haydar after the formal reception, we spend a week here first.'

What was he doing? Xavian's mouth was moving, calm words were being spoken, yet his mind was racing—he was committing himself to six weeks: a week in the desert, a week here, a month in Haydar. Six weeks with her…six weeks when it should have been two…six weeks with this woman who had so boldly challenged him…six weeks with a woman who had not lowered her eyes, who even now dared to hold his gaze as she responded in soft tones.

'I would be honoured to spend time getting closer to the people of Qusay.'

'Good,' Xavian clipped.

Still she looked at him, and Xavian was sorely tempted to pull back the veil, to see his bride, to reveal the woman who would be his bedfellow for the next few weeks. But of course, he did not. Instead he opened the door, and again Akmal practically fell into the room.

'I trust you heard that?' Xavian said. 'We shall remain in Qusay for a week after the reception, then the Queen and I will be in Haydar for a month. You can release that information with the wedding photo.'

Layla gave a brief nod and then walked out of the room. Xavian stood, his back ramrod-straight, his jaw grinding together, as she paused and addressed Akmal.

'You will bring the new release to me for approval after it has been worded.' Briefly she turned back to Xavian. 'I like to check all press statements personally...I am sure you are the same.'

Xavian was still smarting even as the helicopter lifted to take them deep into the desert. How dared she walk into his chambers and make demands so boldly? How dared she tell him what was wise? How dared she speak as if she were his equal? Why, he was King of Qusay—King of a rich, prosperous land that produced both oil and rare emeralds, a progressive land where the people flourished under strong leadership. It was her country that needed him—the people of Haydar who needed strong leadership to guide them out of the Dark Ages! His voice that she needed to quell the rising unrest.

He was annoyed with himself too—for offering her an explanation, for engaging with her. He did not particularly want a wife, and certainly he did not want anyone close.

His own company was enough to be dealing with now.

And he *hadn't* apologised!

He was tempted to tap her on the shoulder and tell her that.

The golden expanse of sand stretching beneath did nothing to soothe him. Xavian was seriously rattled now, and ready to remind her of her place. Baja, her senior lady-in-waiting was accompanying them in the helicopter, and he could feel her silent disapproval as he took his new wife's hand, pleasantly surprised by the slender, pale fingers that he held in his, admiring the manicured nails. For the first time he actually looked forward to the unveiling, to finding out what was in the package that awaited him.

'A feast awaits us,' Xavian said, smiling to himself as she blinked her lowered lashes. Then he leant towards her and watched as her eyes squeezed together in the first display of nervousness he had seen. And that gave him pleasure too, so he elaborated slightly. 'And after we have eaten, another feast awaits.'

The desert staff came out to greet them, and to lay a long roll of carpet from where the helicopter landed to the tented abode. Of course there were more staff than usual, for not only was it a honeymoon, but Layla's own maidens were there to greet the royal couple as well.

Seeing her jewelled slippers there by his as he entered the desert palace gave the place an unfamiliar air. Usually Xavian came to the desert to be alone—oh, occasionally he would summon a mistress, but this was his place for retreat, and he wasn't sure how he felt about sharing it. But share he must—on this occasion at least.

He was married.

Tiny bells were strewn along the tent walls and from the ceilings of all the corridors, to give the honeymooners ample warning of approaching servants, and they tinkled now as the royal couple made their way deep into the heart of his desert abode. The air was fragrant with incense, petals were strewn on the thick Persian rugs that covered the soft floor, and as a heavy silk drape was parted Xavian watched as she stepped into the main living space. It was traditionally decorated—rugs adorned the tent walls, and there were low sofas covered with richly coloured cushions and velvet throws—but it was lavishly decorated too, with intricate carvings and musical instruments, and golden antique mirrors that glistened and twinkled, reflecting the soft candlelight and oil lamps. There was a low table set for them with solid gold plates and cups decorated with rare gems, and the dishes were laden with a delectable wedding night feast as Qusay's most skilled musician softly played the *qanoon*.

It was perfect—so why, Xavian pondered, did she make no comment?

Perhaps she was feeling overwhelmed? Xavian conceded. Perhaps she was worried that the Haydar royal desert abode would look meagre beside this splendour? Or perhaps, Xavian realised as Baja approached and Layla stood rigid and tense, she was worried about revealing herself to her husband?

She had his full attention!

Xavian stood silently watching as Baja helped his new bride out of the golden layers that swathed her body. As the many layers were unwound Xavian found he was holding his breath in anticipation, realising that he had woefully misjudged the figure that was slowly being revealed to him. Oh, there were curves, but they were ripe, feminine curves that enchanted him. He walked slowly around her, admiring her as he did so. Tonight would not be such a hardship after all. She was dressed in a knee-length, heavily jewelled golden dress that hugged her womanly flesh, and her skin was incredibly pale—even for a royal Haydarn. Her slender ankles had been hennaed for him—tiny auburn flowers coiled up from her feet, leading the gaze upwards along her calves. Only there was no time to ponder and savour, for Baja was now removing the veil that covered Layla's face, and for a second Xavian was lost as his wife was exposed to him.

She was shockingly beautiful.

Far, far more exquisite than even he could have dreamt.

Thick raven hair tumbled long and curling, down her back and over her creamy shoulders, framing her delicate face. Her cheeks were softly rouged, her lips plump and delectable, and there was a slight tremble to them that was the only hint to her nervousness. So enchanting, so delicate, so feminine was she that Xavian actually wondered if he had misinterpreted her harsh words earlier—clearly he had misunderstood, for surely nothing but sweetness could come from those lips?

He offered his hand to guide her to the prepared table, but she demurred. 'I would like to look around.'

'Of course,' Xavian amicably agreed; she was overwhelmed, he told himself, overwhelmed at the thought not just of dining with him, but the *feast* that would follow. 'I will show you.' But she was already walking through his desert abode, and, despite her stunning looks, Xavian felt his irritation rising as she checked and questioned everything.

Her gorgeous eyes narrowed as she turned to Baja.

'Where is my computer?'

As the elderly woman apologised for the oversight, Xavian had had enough.

'It is your honeymoon; surely you were not expecting to work…?'

'Oh?' She turned, her eyes glittering, that full mouth holding the position of that short word, and it was all Xavian could look at: lush lips that he wished would stay silent, a mouth he wanted to feed with the fruits at his table and then thoroughly kiss. But instead that mouth again challenged him. 'I didn't realise we were to spend the whole week getting to know each other…' She gave a questioning smile. 'I understood you wanted time in the desert…'

'Of course I will spend my days in the desert,' Xavian clipped. 'It is right that I spend time with the land and that I ask for its wise counsel.'

'And am I expected to join you?' Just a hint of a frown marred her creamy brow. 'I would be happy to…'

'No!' Xavian had to force his voice not to be husky, appalled at the very thought. 'That time is for reflection, alone.'

'I see.' She gave a brief nod, as if to thank him, then turned to Baja.

'In that case I want my computer.'

'The helicopter has already left,' a servant said, then hastily added, 'Your Highness.'

'Good.' She withered the bold servant with a stare. 'Then it will reach the palace soon— have it return immediately with my computer. After all…' again she gave Xavian a smile '…I can hardly be expected to lounge around here doing nothing all day while my husband takes counsel from the land—I have a kingdom to run.'

She knew she appeared aloof, knew she was being a royal pain—but that was her plan. Better that than reveal her true feelings, for Layla was, in fact, beyond nervous—terrified would be a better description of how she was feeling. The whole day had been spent on a knife-edge, standing in the palace gardens as the minutes had ticked by and still her groom had not shown. He did not want this marriage, and today's lateness had just confirmed his low opinion of her. How she had wished she were in a position to walk away herself.

All this she had thought as she stood there in the palace gardens, mortified beneath her veil and angry too, and then he had appeared suddenly—the man she would marry finally standing beside her as her reluctant groom—and mortification and anger had been replaced with trepidation. Oh, she had known he was good-looking, had heard about his wild reputation with women, and when the wedding had been announced she had been nervous, as any woman would, at the prospect of losing her virginity to such a reputedly formidable lover...

But, then he had been beside her.

There had been flurry as he'd arrived, whipping up the air as he moved to stand next to her, and then it had settled—only dif-

ferently, to a new atmosphere: the tangy
bergamot scent of him, the imposing height
and his presence, his absolute male presence.
And her anger and mortification had been
replaced with a different disquiet at *all* a
marriage entailed, at what so imminently lay
ahead, and *that* moment was almost here!

She walked through to the sleeping
chamber, but her throat was tight and at the
sight of the vast bed she looked away, pulling
at a drape and looking instead into the
bathroom where she would be prepared for
him. Mirrors were everywhere, and a large
bath was in the centre, with stools at the side
from where the maidens would wash her.

'Would you like me to show you the
gardens now?' His sarcasm actually brought
her first genuine smile.

'I admired your beautiful sand as we
landed,' Layla responded with her own
humour, even as Baja frowned, clearly not
getting the joke. 'It must take a lot of work
to keep it looking so fine.'

'Hours!' Xavian said, rolling his eyes, and
she wanted to laugh. But she checked herself.
This was no time to let down her guard; she
*had* to set the tone.

No matter that he was the most sensual, breathtakingly beautiful man she had ever seen, no matter that this was the man who would share her body and her bed, and no matter that she wanted to turn tail and run at the imposing sight of him. It was imperative she stay in control and state her intentions right from the very start.

A passive queen she might appear to her people, but if Xavian thought she would quietly acquiesce, he must quickly realise his wife had a voice!

'Now we will eat.' Xavian broke into her thoughts with his clear order—so clear Layla realised it would be petty to argue. 'Our wedding feast awaits.'

She sat at the low table, her knees towards him, her feet behind, as a discreet servant filled two heavy gold cups with a rich sweet nectar. She knew from her readings, and from Baja's teachings, what it was: a thick, unique strain of honey that had been mixed with twenty ground almonds and one hundred pine nuts to aid in arousal. To that rare mix ground poppyseeds had been added, to foster disinhibition, and it would be fed to them each night in the desert, as was the correct way. She let him feed her the potent brew that promised him her full arousal, and had to gulp the sticky liquid as he poured it quickly, too quickly for her taut throat and mouth. Some trickled down her chin, and her fingers caught the stray droplets. Because she must drink each last drop, as was the rule, she licked her fingers clean and realised she was shaking—realised, as she picked up the cup to feed Xavian his share of the potion, that she did not want to.

Didn't want to feed him or his ardour,

He was *so* male.

And soon she would be glad of that, Layla reminded herself. Soon, she would be grateful that her chosen mate had such an excellent physique, that the man who would be her only lover, who would father her children and give her Haydar's heirs, was such a fine specimen.

She just had to get this night over with— had to see for the first time a naked man, had to perform her wifely duty—and one day soon, Layla told herself, his body, his maleness, would not scare her so; one day soon, she promised herself, this would no longer be foreign.

The seated musician was still gently

playing the *qanoon*, skilfully plucking the strings far slower than her rapid heartbeat. The harp-like music was filling the tent and inflaming her nerves.

She held the cup to his mouth and poured the brew tentatively, watching him swallow, fearing those lips that would soon be on hers and that body that would soon be pressed to her own.

She was dizzy with a fear born of too many nights alone. Baja had told her a little of what to expect and would, she had promised, tell her more when she prepared her.

He finished his potion and she remained by his side.

As was correct.

The wedding feast had been carefully prepared. Far from the lavish feast that would adorn the tables at their formal reception, this was a light, thoughtfully chosen meal for a bridal couple, so their bellies would not be full and their senses would still be sharp. It consisted of sweet, succulent fruits that would give energy and promote fertility, and was to be eaten with their fingers.

There was no conversation, just eyes watching and waiting as they fed each other—once he leant forward, so close she could feel the heat from his skin as he pushed back her hair so she could eat the sticky fruit, and she felt her stomach tighten in anticipation of all that was to come. He inhaled her scent and she felt his breath on her neck, just a cool dust of a breeze, and the fear that was rising within tipped into something different. A strange flutter of excitement was stirring deep inside—tonight she would know, tonight, it would be revealed: the secret, the reward, the answer she had sought on those lonely, empty nights.

Small dishes were offered, eaten, and then removed, till the table was bare. It would be time soon. She watched as he parted a pomegranate and offered her half. The tiny beaded seeds were sweet on her tongue, but still her head was spinning. The scent of musk was having a giddying effect, and the *qanoon*'s notes were more urgent now. She drank mint tea so her mouth would be fresh for him, and his eyes roamed her body, lingering on her breasts, which felt heavy now. She had never been more aware of them. Safely hidden behind robes, she rarely gave them a thought, but now they ached under his languishing scrutiny. And then his eyes slowly moved along the flood of pink that swept up her chest and neck, that warmed her cheeks. His eyes met and held hers, and she didn't know how to breathe. Her tongue felt too slow, too taut as it bobbed out to moisten dry lips, and she was flooded with the urge for his mouth to claim hers, to taste not the fruit but him.

She was, Xavian realised, ready.

And then it was time, and she wished she could have stayed at the table for a little while longer, wished he had kissed her, wished the night was not so formal, wished they were alone. Because for just a moment or two she had had her first glimpse of arousal. His rare beauty, the unique scent of him, the bold way he had looked at her, made her greedy with a sudden need for more—except Baja was leading her away for bathing as Xavian headed to the bed, and never had her terror been more acute, but never had she been so excited.

Part of her wanted to run out to the desert, to flee, but now she found she wanted the moment too. She no longer wanted it over with, because her body was curious in a different way, because out of the circle of his aura her heart and senses were fading to near normal—and she was sure it had nothing to do with the fruits or the poppyseeds.

In the bathroom the maidens bathed and oiled her. She had been hennaed for him in Haydar: apart from the trail of flowers coiling over her ankles and hands, low on her stomach there was a butterfly, and she shuddered with the sudden thought of that decadent mouth there…

Only Baja was telling her to expect something different.

There would be perhaps a perfunctory kiss, Baja explained as she climbed out of the scented bath and the maidens readied her, and then the King would take care of everything. She would lift her nightgown, more oil would be by the bed, and hopefully the King would use it. If not the bath she had lain in was loaded with oil, so she would be soft and tender.

It would not take long, Baja assured her. Two, maybe three thrusts to take her virginity. And because the King would be unsheathed, and after the potent food, and with the heady rose and musk in which she had bathed, it would be over with quickly.

But Layla wanted more—wanted more of what she had glimpsed at his table.

'Should I touch him…?' Layla asked. She was a perfectionist, good at everything, and suddenly she wanted to be a good lover for her husband too. But Baja just laughed, and even the maidens giggled. Oh, they knew all about King Xavian and his endless women. Gossip amongst palace staff was rife, even if the kingdoms were separated by miles. Baja had a cousin who worked in the royal chambers at the Qusay palace, and knew there were lovers ready and waiting to step in as soon as Layla was safely home and the King back in his palace.

Layla's body was needed for one reason only; she did not have to worry herself with such things!

'His mistresses will take care of all *that* for you.' Baja was attempting to reassure her, but her words were hailstones on Layla's warm body. Cold and stinging, they forced a new emotion: jealousy, for the unknown faces that would take care of her husband's most private needs. 'Don't worry, Your Highness,' Baja continued, calling her by her title, as she always did in front of the maidens. 'It will be just once or twice a month till you're impregnated that you must suffer his attentions, and then you can rest for a year at least.'

A nightdress was slipped over her damp, oiled body, her hair brushed and her lips rouged, and then she was declared ready.

She parted the flimsy drapes and walked into his chamber.

Oil lamps and candles lit the room; the vast low bed was decorated with sheer organza. The *qanoon* was still being played in the main area of the tent, breaking the silence of the desert, its soft seductive notes meant to ease her passage to his arms.

He was on the bed—naked, she was sure, beneath the silken sheet that covered his lower half. He was just as impressive out of uniform. His broad chest and long muscular arms would make light work for the palace tailor, for his masculinity did not need enhancing. There were dark scars around his wrist. At first, in the candlelight, Layla thought he had been hennaed too, but, no, they were scars. But it was not her place to notice, so instead she looked up at him, watched as his arrogant, haughty face softened a touch as she walked towards him.

She wished for a moment that she *was* his lover, not his wife.

The oil was making her nightgown cling to her body as she climbed in bed beside him.

'Don't be nervous.'

'I'm not,' Layla said, except she was shivering.

He kissed her. She felt his lips press on hers and his tongue slide in, and she tried to kiss him back, her mouth moving, copying his.

As a princess there had been no kisses, no anything, and she ached for more experience, felt embarrassed by her innocence. She couldn't enjoy his kiss, could only feel the long, solid length of his manhood pressing into her thigh, and the size of him made her dizzy. She prayed that he would oil her.

She lifted her nightdress.

'There is no rush…' He pulled his head back; he wanted to keep kissing her, for her to relax, for her to at least try and enjoy this royal duty.

'I would prefer it to be over,' came her stilted voice.

So would he, then, Xavian thought—while

wondering if it would be poor form to summon a mistress on his honeymoon.

He loved sex. Too much was never enough for Xavian, and he was always ready. But this hard-nosed businesswoman, who had come to his bed for such a clinical mating, was nothing like the lush female he had fed and prepared. Frankly, if that was her wish, he wanted it over too!

He *was* considerate. He dipped his fingers in the gold dish by the bed and smeared her tender pink flesh. Feeling the sweet warmth, he hardened further, his finger gliding past her pearl, his duty done,

Layla saw what had already appeared ominously large grow some more, and her throat was tight. She could feel his hand down *there,* and she saw him, so hard and erect she almost felt sick. He saw her looking, saw that mix of terror and fascination, and his finger lingered, pressed her pretty place and stroked it for a moment, felt the hard nub of her clitoris and stroked it some more.

She wanted to close her legs, didn't want him touching her. It felt wrong and it just heightened her nervousness—this sex, this touching, this sharing that he would later do with someone else!

'Now you will oil me.' He liked stroking her, liked the feel of her moisture meeting his fingers, and she could feel the small, insistent pads of pressure that made her stomach flurry as she dipped her shaking fingers in the bowl.

Baja hadn't warned her of this, hadn't warned her that her fingers should be silky and oily too. She didn't want to touch him there, but perhaps it would help her later. She made herself do it, her fingers tentative, a quick sheen of oil on his long length, and averted her eyes from his gargoylic impressive proportions. But involuntarily her gaze returned. It felt so different from how it looked—which was hard and angry. But the skin beneath her fingers was soft, like rich velvet.

'More…'

Still he was stroking her. Her stomach felt heavy, her thighs did too, and she didn't like it—didn't like these strange feelings. She wanted her more familiar control, so she ended this pointless diversion—she was at her most fertile; the wedding had been arranged around her cycle. The way she responded to him unnerved her—the unfamiliar reaction of her senses, the strange weakening that he wrought in her mind. It was time to be brave, time for it to be over, time to reclaim her head.

'Now.' She moved his hand from her private place and lay down. 'Do it now.'

Xavian was tired of her games. He had felt her unfurl for a second, yet she refused to relent, to enjoy his caress.

He had hoped for more from a wife, but had expected less.

Shame, though, because she *was* beautiful—her body full and ripe, her hair dark. And those lips could kiss if they would just learn; that body could know pleasure if she would only allow it.

'Take off your nightgown...' Xavian said, because he needed something to help him along. She did as she was told and it certainly helped that she was so good-looking, Xavian thought, as he lowered himself on to her and she duly parted her legs—and all help was gratefully received as he did his duty with this beautiful plank of wood.

Xavian was nervous.

For the first time ever with a woman there was just a beat of trepidation as he nudged her entrance without the familiar barrier. He pictured her body to keep himself hard, and lowered his head for a moment to suck on her breast, to taste her ripe flesh for his own benefit. Yet still as he tried to coax a response from her, there was none.

Layla, now the moment had come, was terrified. She could not show him that, of course—could never show anyone her private fears. She was Queen: always in control, always assured.

He could feel the tears on her face as his cheek pressed next to hers. He was nudging at her entrance, and really he knew she wanted it over, that despite her silent tears this had to be done, and he was angry.

Angry at her refusal to even try and enjoy it, angry at her martyred ways, at her urging him to just do it when he had wanted to kiss, had wanted pleasure not just for himself but for her.

A rare tenderness crept in at the last moment—it wasn't just the salt of her tears that moved him, nor her beauty that made him question his duty, it was her.

That glimpse of her he had seen at his table, and just for a moment in his bed.

But, more than that, it was the woman who had marched into his room and told him to do better that intrigued him. She had insisted on better from him, and he wanted better for her.

That bristling, angry woman, he realised, was nervous, and for Xavian there was rare guilt too.

She had kept herself for him.

Of course she had. There could be no other way. Without question he must take a virgin as his bride.

But by his refusal to commit for years he had denied her this pleasure. Denied her comfort, denied her solace up until this point. For Xavian, that was all that sex was. A place where he climbed out of his mind, where he escaped, where he *lived* for a moment, an hour, a night.

He could give that to her too—if she would just relent.

He had a brief glimpse of a different future—a future that could be hers if she would just take it. A place that was for them. He wanted her to see it too, wanted duty and conformity to vanish, wanted the solace he was finding tonight to spread to her.

'It doesn't have to be like this.' At the last minute he faltered, tasted her tears with his lips and tried to breathe life into a pointless death. 'It does not have to be duty.' And then his mouth pressed her salty cheek and tried to offer comfort—except she turned her face away.

She could not explain her tears, except to tell him that Baja's words had stung.

What was the point of intimacy, of giving herself to him, when there would be others?

'Your lovers can writhe for you,' Layla choked. 'Let them be the ones to tell you how wonderful you are—I just want it over.'

'Why would I take a lover?' Xavian said into her ear. He was in just a little way, could feel the resistance of her innocence despite her bold and snarling demeanour.

'Because that is what you will do… I will be in Haydar; you will be here…'

Ah, so she was jealous already. Xavian smiled in triumph, yet something inside him that sought comfort in her assumption that he would take a lover was shifting as he held her in his arms.

She was a queen.

He held a woman who was on his level.

And not just in title. She challenged him, and curiously Xavian wanted more of her.

All of her, perhaps?

Which meant she needed more of him.

'Why would we need lovers...' his mouth was on the shell of her ear '...if we satisfy each other...?' He had taken himself from her centre now, and his one hand was playing with her bottom, the other working at her breast. Then he moved his head to her nipple, sucked it again, and she stared down at it, watched as his tongue flicked and his lips blew. 'We have a fleet of planes at our disposal, and there is always...' he looked up, black eyes glinting '...the phone.'

She gave a shocked giggle at the thought of whispering on the phone to him whilst in her bed at night, startled by her excitement at the games they could play, at the fact that they could make their own lives, that Baja's ways and the ways of old didn't have to be so.

'It is my duty to satisfy you, Layla.' He took her breast deep in his mouth and suckled hard, till she squirmed in heady pleasure. 'And, despite my earlier display, I do take my duties seriously—you will not want to stray...'

'Stray?'

'If I am less than a husband should be…' Xavian said, smug in the knowledge of his prowess, dragging his tongue lower as she shivered beneath him, licking the little butterfly that had been painted for his pleasure and feeling the soft curve of her stomach on his cheek.

Layla realised that he was giving the same rules to her! She knew that it happened—her sister Noor was married to a prince who was impotent for women and Noor was allowed to take a discreet lover… It *was* different being married, but her sister was a princess; Layla was Queen—why would she need a lover?

He was back now, his fingers stroking her more firmly as still he kissed her stomach, telling her with his hands and mouth that it was her right to be fulfilled—taking her to a new world, sharing with her the secret that this, *this* was her right. And then his head moved down and he kissed a different butterfly, and he knew that she was his.

How he loved women.

How he loved feeling them unfurl in his hands. But his pleasure had never been greater as Layla's cynicism melted beneath his lips. His tongue flicked her clitoris and he could feel the tremor in her thighs, hear the little sighs that told him she was ready. But he wanted his kiss—wanted that mouth that had teased him with fruit, that had spoken such brittle words, to be soft under his. So he kissed her again, and this time she kissed him back.

He chased her tongue with his, caught it and sucked on it, then took her lips and sucked them too. And then he kissed her so hard and so deep, her breasts flattened by his chest, her legs coiling around his, his fingers lost in knots of her hair. He almost forgot her innocence as his body led him into her, to her unique gift, because Layla was desperate for him, willing him on. He pressed into her guarded place and she was ready for him— urgently, desperately ready... She sobbed as he seared into her, and aghast at his own ferocity, at the fear that he had been too urgent, he lifted his head, saw her tears and berated himself—except she was unleashed beneath him and it was as if she were free, as if somehow he had set her free, because her lips were on his cheek now, her fingers pressing him in, slowly at first, but with every tentative thrust she begged him in deeper, with every move of his body she rose for more.

'It is over…' Baja had been pacing, but hearing her mistress's cry she sat down with the handmaidens, proud of her Queen and glad for her that this long night was over. Except the cries continued, and the handmaidens were sitting with their head lowered, the youngest's face a burning blush, as Baja attempted to reassure her. 'It will be over soon…'

Layla wanted it never to be over.

While having been told what to expect, still she had privately dreamt how this night might be—but neither Baja's dour predictions, nor the flightiest of her own dreams came close to the bliss of reality! Awkward kisses, clumsy motions had been replaced by this rush—a rush of sensations, feelings, of Xavian sweeping her into this unfamiliar place where all she was was herself, a better self, an unguarded self, a woman in his arms. And he held her as he filled her, brought from her involuntary noises, and the bliss of him inside her was unsurpassed—until the next moment. For just as she accepted the new sensation of Xavian inside her things changed again. As he moved within her she felt swathed, wrapped, cosseted, and even at her most vulnerable, with him inside her, his skin sliding over hers, his breath harsh and ragged in her ear, even as he took her to a new, dangerous and unfamiliar place, she felt absolutely secure. Her thighs ached, her stomach pulled tight, and his cheek was next to hers. All she could hear was his breath as he moved slowly, and though there was no yardstick for her to measure by, there was a need now in Layla for Xavian to move faster, for him to match the sudden urgency of her body. She felt her hips rising in demand, yet he refused to relent—if anything he moved slower, deeper, as her body pleaded for him to join her.

His entrance had hurt, a brief, searing hurt, yet now, as he moved slowly, it was a different hurt, almost an ache. Like a kiss to thin air she said his name, pleading when she had never had to beg before. Layla hardly recognised her own voice, this sob, this whimper from usually assured lips, but she cried out as a rush of heat flared through her body. Her hands dug into his back as she demanded that he join her, and yet he did not, even as she gave in and shuddered beneath him. Her cries went unmatched; he was seemingly impervious to the writhing of her body, and still he moved within...

Triumph coursed through him as he rocked deep within her, as he felt her dissolve beneath him, heard the cries of her assent. And he wanted to join her, to tip into oblivion, but the climb to the summit was wondrous. Here the air was clearer, the sounds more vivid, the colours brighter, and he wanted to linger, to find the answer to what would happen if he stayed, if he lingered, if he ventured on to an uncharted place...

He kissed her for sustenance, took her weary, shocked lips in his and confirmed his intent. And then he told her, stared into the lusty black of her pupils and showed her a different way.

'*This* is how it could be.'

She had thought her body spent, yet it was nowhere near. The languorous, slow love-making he had teased her with before was replaced, and the urgent, demanding pressure she had sought earlier was given to her now. He was relentless, his arms wrapped around her, his face smothering hers, kissing her eyes, her mouth, her face, her ears, driving deep into her as her hips rose to a rhythm that matched his. And she was crying and pleading, because it was as close to the edge as she ever wanted to venture, yet she wanted to be there all the same. Scared to jump, to fall, she wanted to roll back at the last minute, to save herself—except Xavian had just gone, his body moving fast and then stilling as he released, and it ripped through her like lightning. She had an image then, as if he were offering her his hand, and instead of rolling away she took it, jumped with him to a place of freedom where she could scream out his name as her body spasmed while he emptied into her, her feminine muscles pulsing in perfect time with his. And then he caught her, with soft, deep strokes that brought her slowly back to her senses, that soothed her twitching body to a new state of calm.

A peaceful calm like one she had never witnessed.

All the heat was fading, their glistening bodies cooling as he kissed her back to the world, and then he said it again.

'This is how it could be.'

## CHAPTER THREE

Xavian rarely slept.

Of course he slept—it would be impossible not to and live—but even in sleep part of him remained alert, watching out for the dreams that plagued him and staving them off. He was too proud to let his lovers see his distress, but lovers were easily disposed of. Not so easily his wife on their wedding night.

He had been determined to remain vigilant even in sleep, deciding he would rest properly during his days in the desert. He would sleep deeply for a while in the shelter of a canyon he knew well so that he could stay on guard by night—yet for the first time in many nights, and certainly for the first time with a woman in his bed, sleep—real sleep—overcame him.

He could smell her scent, feel her soft

body beside him, but it was more than that. Their lovemaking had been like a balm—never before had he felt so replete—and though he had held her in the crook of his arm, though his intention had been just to doze, his subconscious dictated otherwise…

It beckoned him onwards, and foolishly he followed, but then sense took over and he resisted for a moment, fought to open his eyes. It beckoned again. It was actually a compliment that he turned his back to her—that for the first time with a woman Xavian truly rested.

There was the soft sound of bells, the comfort of her presence, and this strange beckoning for him to follow, which he did…

He found himself in a palace.

Not his palace. Perhaps, Xavian thought, it was Haydar? But no, as he stared at the pictures on the walls somehow he knew this was not a dream, but a memory.

He could hear the unfamiliar sound of true uninhibited laughter, and it came from a child that looked like him.

There was a bird!

A tiny silver bird had swooped into the palace and all was in chaos.

He was running, laughing, cheering in delight as he chased it through the corridors.

Glee was filling him as the maids ran with brooms and tried to corner it, but the bird just soared, flapping its wings and swooping, taunting them almost, and how it made him laugh—a laugh that came from within, a surge of joy filling him with pure joy, an innocent pleasure that warmed and flooded his usually cold veins.

An unadulterated joy such as he had never known.

But he felt it now.

Even as he was scolded.

He could feel the gap his baby teeth had left while he grinned at a face that should not be familiar, though his soul recognised her as his mother as she told him to go outside.

He loved this dream—he loved this place, this palace, where children were still laughing.

He loved the feel of Layla's fingers on his shoulders and moving down his arms, the whisper of her breath on his back as she stayed with him while he dreamed on.

There was a beach, with water and fun and the sheer freedom of the ocean, and still the feel of Layla's gentle fingers on his wrist—and then innocence ended. That safe, childish world was terminated as he met for the first time with fear. Real fear that ripped through his body and stole his youth in a matter of seconds.

There was blood in the water and hell in his soul, and his heart raced and his mind willed him back to the real world. He was stuck in a dream and he insisted he awoke—because the sheets would soon be drenched with his sweat, and he knew in a moment he would scream.

Now, now he must awake—before she witnessed his truth. But it was already out: a shout filling the silent night, his body rigid, the pounding of his heart, and then something unexpected.

The nightmare was all too familiar; what was unexpected was the comfort of her arms, the press of her lips on the back of his neck and the strange invasion of calm.

Layla had heard the bells fade as Baja and the maidens retreated to the servants' quarters and they were left truly alone.

The marriage had been consummated.

Duty done.

Layla had never shared a bed—and though her body was tired, her mind was all too aware of the man beside her.

He had been holding her, but had turned away as sleep came. His back was towards her and she could hear his soft breathing, hear winds that were unfamiliar.

Each desert brought different songs; she had learnt that long ago—the vast planes and dunes and canyons delivered their own tune, and the Qusay Desert sang loudly now as she tried to block it out and sleep.

He really was beautiful.

Even asleep, even with his back towards her, even in the dark, she could sense his rare beauty—and he had had made her braver than she could have imagined. Because she didn't resist when the urge hit. She reached out and ran her fingers along his shoulders, felt the muscle beneath the smooth skin, and she yearned for him to turn over, to hold her again, but he was deeply asleep—his breathing regular and slow—and he didn't move at all at her touch.

So she was a little braver.

Tracing her path down his arm, and then to his wrist, she could feel the thick scars beneath her fingers, almost feel the pain, and then she felt him stir and quickly pulled her hand away, aware that she had intruded.

And then, from nowhere, the storm gathered and hit.

His fear was so immediate, so palpable, that for an instant Layla truly thought something had happened—something real, something so terrible that in a second she would see it too—like an earthquake, or a fire, or an intruder. As the tension ripped through him, as his heart raced and his body jerked, she expected him to leap from the bed, for the threat to become apparent.

All this was processed in seconds, and then came his shout, and realisation hit her.

His fear was real—the threat was present—but only for Xavian.

It was then she realised he was trapped in a nightmare, and she knew he would not want her to witness it, knew in that second that the polite thing to do would be to turn over, to pretend she had slept through his pain, that his shout had not roused her, to feign sleep when he sat up and turned on the light—but instead she held him.

She said not a word, just held him, kissed

him gently on the back of his icy cold neck, held him till his heart slowed down, till his breathing calmed. and Layla knew that she held not just Xavian, but a secret.

A secret that must not be discussed.

A secret that was Xavian's alone until he chose to share it.

# CHAPTER FOUR

HE COULD not look her in the eye in the morning.

His slight headache would be relieved by coffee, but he felt embarrassed, ashamed, and he did not like those feelings.

As the maids came in and prepared the room for breakfast, he glanced over and watched a blush spread over her cheeks as the lamps were lit and she sat up and they fixed her pillows. The blush did not go as they placed a breakfast table over their laps spread with delicacies—fruits, yoghurts, delicate pastries, honeyed milk, coffee and jugs of fragrant tea. He was sure she was embarrassed that he had shouted out, but he blinked in surprise when, after the maids left, she clapped her hand over her mouth and let out a giggle. Her eyes widened in surprise as she admitted she *was* embarrassed—only it had nothing to do with his dream.

'They bathe me, they dress me...' She knew all that, yet she was still cringing that she was naked under the sheet with him, that the air was heavy with the scent of their love-making, and all she knew was what she said. 'I don't like them coming in here.'

He didn't either.

She blushed again, but for a different reason, as he removed the table, climbed out of bed and stood naked before her.

'What do you want to eat?'

She frowned at his question.

'Pastry.'

'And to drink?'

'The sweet milk.'

She watched as he wrapped a robe around his hips, took the milk and coffee jug and the tiny cups off the tray and placed them by the bedside table. He took off the pastries and placed the plates on the bed and then, for surely the first time, the King cleared the table.

He carried the table outside, and she could hear the bells ringing as he took it along the tent corridor, then he returned, removed the robe and climbed back into the bed.

She knew what would happen.

She heard the bells again—Baja, no doubt, rushing to see what might be the matter—and then she heard his low, firm voice.

'We are not to be disturbed.'

She could picture Baja, standing frozen, because the bells were silent for a moment, and then she scurrying off, and then there was just the sound of the table being taken and, Layla realised, they were truly alone.

'This is our place.' She looked over to him, looked him right in the eye, and now he could look at her there too, as she told him that here was a place for them—a place they could just be—and he was infinitely grateful for her lack of questions, of any need for an explanation as to what had occurred last night, so, so grateful for her unexpected acceptance.

'So you have six sisters?'

He was lying on his side, drinking coffee and eating nothing. Layla sat up in bed and gulped sweet honeyed milk, devoured thick pastries. Breakfast had lasted for ages, just being with her and telling stupid stories—stories he had never shared before, because really there was no one he could share with. Like how Akmal listened at doors, how the name Akmal meant 'perfect' and Akmal thought that he was! Stupid stories, perhaps, except they were thoughts never before shared, little stories never before deemed important, and suddenly now they were.

'Do you get on?'

'Sometimes.' Layla laughed. 'But never all at the same time!' She saw his confused frown. 'Always I am talking to one or two and not talking to one or two others, yet always we are worrying about one another—right now they are probably all worrying about me.'

'Why?'

'Because I am here…' He watched as her hunger vanished, watched the pastry that had been relished return to its jewelled plate. 'They need not worry, of course. They know you are a good provider and that you will be a good husband and give me heirs.' She gave a tight smile and turned her violet eyes to him. 'They have no need for concern. I would though, from my husband, prefer more.'

She broke the mould in so many ways.

She challenged him, she satisfied him, and she offered him something else—something Xavian was fast realising came rarely to a King and must have long been rare for her too...

Conversation.

Real conversation that could not be over-ridden by status. A mind and a voice that could not be swayed by title.

Never—not once, not even for a moment—had he expected that his bride, his duty, the confines of being King, would bring him this.

This...

It was an honour to be King, of course.

From shooting, to deportment, to military prowess, he was the most honoured, he had been told.

The one.

The chosen.

And yet as he'd shot down a clay pigeon, and then a falcon, and then proved himself in combat, honour had had no meaning. Over and over he had been told how he felt, told who he was and told how to be.

Last night, though, he had felt chosen for himself.

And she wanted more. Xavian, though,

was not sure he could give something that he did not know.

Himself.

'Do you wish you had brothers?'

He shook his head. 'It is a waste to wish for something you cannot change—anyway, I have three cousins—we played a bit as children…they are like brothers.'

'One is Kareef?' Layla checked, because she knew a little of his cousins. 'Do you see him much?'

'He is busy ruling Qais. We talk occasionally.'

'And the middle one?'

'Rafiq,' Xavian went on quickly. There were still some things that were not up for discussion. 'He is a businessman, always working, travelling.' She saw his slight, uncomfortable swallow. 'I do not see Tahir,' he said, before she asked, so that the subject could be changed. 'He has been gone for some time…'

'Then they are not like brothers.' Layla said. 'Or rather, not brothers you are close to.'

'As I said,' Xavian said tartly, 'you cannot miss what you do not know.'

'I cannot imagine not having my sisters to

talk to,' she whispered, questioning the wisdom of being too honest. 'Of course there *are* things I would not dare tell them…Baja knows some…'

"Like what?'

She shook her head, but his curiosity was piqued now.

'What does Baja know that you cannot tell your sisters?'

'Nothing.' If he would not give more, then neither would she! Layla had forgotten her own rules—last night's poppyseeds had made her tongue loose, and she bit on it to will it quiet.

'Tell me…'

'No.'

'You can…'

'I can't.'

'You could.'

Yet still she hesitated, her true feelings too volatile to share just yet, even with the man who was her husband. So she offered him a seed, one she hoped he would treat kindly— just a small seed for now, instead of the vast garden of her mind.

A little seed about a stupid teenage

moment when she had once wondered about a man…a visiting prince. Oh, nothing had happened, save that she had giggled and thought too much about him, but as she told him she braced herself for the sting of his hand on her cheek, as Baja's had done. Yet the sting did not come, just his lips, and then a rare apology for keeping her waiting so long.

And little by little, despite her own rules, she started to trust him.

Layla didn't turn on her laptop—and neither did Xavian wander out to the desert.

The world could wait, because new priorities had been established.

No matter the clinical decisions behind their coupling, their parents—unwittingly, perhaps—had got this so right.

It was no longer just about business.

Baja was beside herself at first. She had feared for her Queen because of this brute who had been imposed upon her. She took the poppyseeds out of their nightly elixir, reduced the quantity of pine nuts, but the potency of the first drinks refused to wear off. Her mistress was almost stupefied—even a couple of mornings later, as she was bathed, Xavian was all Layla could talk about.

'He's wonderful, Baja…' Layla said as a maiden washed her hair. 'We talk about anything.'

'What do you tell him?' Baja checked, her shrewd eyes narrowing.

'Lots of things,' Layla said, her chin jutting out in defiance. 'He is my husband; surely I can trust him with anything?'

'I will finish…' Baja took the jug from the maiden and instructed her to leave, pouring the water over and over Layla's hair just a touch less gently than the maiden had, and Layla could sense Baja's questions. She could feel her tension even before she spoke. 'You know my concern is only for you.'

'I know that,' Layla said, feeling the soapy water sting her eyes, and then Baja's bony fingers rubbing oil into her scalp.

'You are always so careful…'

'I am,' Layla agreed through tight lips.

'Of course you are…' Poor Baja. She tried so hard to choose her words carefully. Even though she had raised Layla since her mother's death, was her only true confidante and could speak to the Queen in ways others would never, still she had to exert caution. 'But he is ruler of another land. His heart belongs to the people of Qusay,' Baja said. 'Always he will put them first.'

'As is right,' Layla said, because her people always had to come first too.

'You have fought hard to lead, Layla,' Baja said, working the oil through long raven locks. 'If the King knew how it wearies you…' She paused for a moment, worked the oil in, before tentatively going on. 'He would, of course, want to help you.'

'I am not going to hand over my kingdom…'

'Of course not. The sapphire mines are plentiful, and you know the good you can do,' Baja said, and Layla closed her eyes.

She knew what Baja was hinting at. Haydar had so much untapped potential, and it was Layla's dream to see her country prosper, to mine wisely, to build hospitals and schools. Would Xavian's dreams be the same? Would his vision be as strong for *her* people?

'He is a powerful King,' Baja mused. 'But a King can never have too much power.'

'I am not going to hand it over…' Layla could blame the tears in her eyes on the sting of the soap. 'But if he knew how it tired me, knew of the burden, surely sharing with my husband—?'

'Secrets are the weapon of men...' Baja interrupted. She had crossed the line and would take the punishment, because she was scared for her Queen and scared for her land. 'Your secrets are his power. Guard them wisely.'

Layla did not chastise Baja, because even if she didn't like what she heard she did value her opinion, and she knew as she sat in the bath and let the oil soak into her hair that the old lady spoke without malice.

She wanted so much for her people. Haydar was her passion, and there was no one who would fight for it in the way that she did—certainly not the King of another land.

Baja was right. It was imperative she separated her heart from her head.

A loving husband, a sensual lover, perhaps a friend too—but maybe Xavian did not need to know all that was in her mind.

As Baja filled a jug to rinse her hair again, she watched the old lady's shoulders stiffen as the drapes were parted and in walked the King.

'Allow me.' He took the jug from Baja and stood till she had left. Layla, wondering if he had heard them talking, sat tense in the still water as Xavian came over and slowly poured the water over her hair.

'You are not supposed to see my preparations.'

'Why?' Xavian asked.

'I should come to you only when I am beautiful.'

'You are beautiful now,' Xavian said, and she was: oiled and wet and warm. How tired he was of protocol, of the maidens, and of the servants who invaded their space, of Baja, who sat in silent guard around her.

'I am sick of the staff,' Xavian admitted broodingly, disrobing and climbing in the bath to join her. 'Sick of Baja hovering, and tired of that *qanoon* playing every night.'

Layla giggled. 'It is tiresome at times.'

'We could dismiss them.'

Layla's eyes widened.

'All of them,' Xavian said. 'We could send them back to the palace…'

'Who would bathe me?' Layla gave a nervous laugh, but his hands answered that.

'Who would prepare our meals?'

'Us.'

'I don't know…' Alone with him, without

Baja to steady her… He was so consuming, so *dangerous* to her principles, that she truly didn't know what to do, so instead she continued to bathe him, as he did the same to her. 'We will tell them to be more discreet,' Layla settled for instead, cupping her hands and pouring water on his tense shoulders. 'I am used to having people around, I guess— you should try having six sisters!' She felt him relax under her tender hands, and he even laughed as she told him more stories about her and her sisters, and the trouble they'd caused their maids as children.

And, in a rare, unguarded moment, he told her some tales too.

'I remember going to my cousins—always they were arguing, fighting. Only sometimes they were laughing… Then I would return to the palace, and it was then that I missed my brothers,' Xavian said, then frowned at the slip of his own tongue and corrected himself. 'It was then that I missed having brothers.'

'So you *can* miss what you have never had!' Layla smiled, glad that he was being more open, even if she was scared to be. 'What about school?' Layla asked. 'Did everyone want to be friends with the future King?'

'I was taught at home.' His black eyes met hers and he was honest. 'Yes, it was lonely.'

He was more tender than passionate, and it was his words that were intimate—thoughts that would bind them closer together. And little by little, despite Baja's warnings, it felt so right that she told him more, trusted him more. Layla even told him about Noor, because soon he would be in Haydar and all the family knew. But there was no raised eyebrow, and his response surprised her.

'Are they happy?'

'Yes.' Layla blinked at his response. 'Ahmed loves Noor in many ways, just not in the intimate way that a  husband should. They had to marry; they have been betrothed since childhood.'

'Like us?'

'Like us.' Layla nodded. 'It is better that Ahmed trusted her with his secret. Now they both have wonderful lives, and their people are happy.'

Xavian was pensive over their lost years. 'Perhaps if we had met sooner, if we had spoken…'

'We have met,' Layla corrected him. 'I

stood beside you in the line-up at the Aristan Coronation. I was hoping you would at least acknowledge me, but after the Queen passed by…' Even now she blushed at the humiliating memory. 'You snubbed me, as I recall.'

'I did not…'

'You did.' Layla choked on the anger that suddenly filled her. She didn't want to probe old wounds, but he had hurt her. 'You looked straight through me.'

'I had other things on my mind that day.'

'Like what?' Still her anger burnt, because that was another year he had denied her. 'What could have been so important that day that you could not turn and smile to your betrothed?'

Her hands were not soothing him now as they worked his tense muscles, and her questions were becoming too intrusive.

'What happened here?' She was trying to change the subject, trying to get over old resentments, so she asked a different question, tracing the thick dark scars around both his wrists with her finger.

'I was sick as a child,' Xavian answered, staring at the familiar scars, and though the water was warm, suddenly he was cold, remembering the reason for his distraction at the coronation, remembering Queen Stefania's eyes widening when she too noticed his scars. Suddenly Xavian felt it imperative that he explain their presence to Layla, and that she believed him. 'I was very sick. I had seizures… They had to tether me to the bed. Sometimes I would become delirious and wander…'

'Oh.' He could see the confusion in her eyes, and not for the first time Xavian was wondering too. 'They tethered you?' Her fingers were soft on the scars, tracing them, examining them just as he did at times, and her mind was surely asking the same questions as his. He had been a royal prince, the heir to the throne—surely there would have been nurses to watch him? Surely there had been no need to tether him? 'What was wrong with you?'

He pulled his wrists away.

'What made you so ill?'

'Does it matter?'

'Perhaps,' Layla challenged. After all, she was to bear his child, yet she had been told none of this. 'What was wrong with you?'

Xavian hauled himself out of the bath, wrapped a cloth around his waist, and found that for the first time since their arrival in the desert he needed his space, needed to be alone—her probing, her questions, were getting on his nerves.

'I am going to the desert today.'

She didn't understand the change in him. He left her shivering in the now tepid water, confused as to what had gone wrong. She wrapped a towel around her body and followed him out to the sleeping chamber, where he dressed unaided.

'I thought we were going to spend time…'

'You do not want to,' Xavian pointed out. 'I suggested we dismiss the staff, take time to get to know each other, but you are concerned with who will prepare your meals…'

'No,' Layla said slowly, certain that wasn't what had upset him so much. It was only when she had asked about the scars that his mood had changed. 'I am not worried about the meals…'

'You are worried about who would bathe you.'

'You said that you would bathe me…'

He was dressed now, in white robes that would reflect the harsh heat and accentuated his dark skin and unshaven jaw. She stood in the bedroom, wrapped in a robe, refusing to just be quiet. 'How long will you be…?'

He laughed then—a mirthless laugh that was unfamiliar to her. 'Why? Are you worried that you might burn the dinner?' The huge tent was too small, her eyes too intense and her presence too invasive. He needed to be out of there. 'I will return when I choose to.'

# CHAPTER FIVE

THE desert helped. Out here in the silence he could breathe, he could think, even if he did not want to.

He had accepted the explanation when, as a child, he had asked his mother about the scars.

'You were such a sick child, Xavian.' Tears had filled her eyes as she'd tried to answer his many questions. 'You were so feeble, so ill—and then, when you were seven, it was like a miracle. Slowly you improved…'

And she had told him about his sickly ways, about the seizures, but always more questions had remained. As a young teenager, clever, curious, he had spoken with the palace doctor as he was about to be taught to desert race in a Jeep.

'Can I drive?'

'Of course.'

'I have seizures…'

'Not for years Xavian,' the doctor had said. 'You grew out of them.'

He walked, for hours he walked, and then he sat—stared at the golden landscape that he ruled—and then he looked down, pulled back the sleeves on his robe and stared at the dark raised scars, turning his wrist over and asking again: who would bind a royal Prince with rope?

He could *feel* the rope. He sat there and the desert was more patient than his parents, because it let him ask rather than silence him.

Here he could think, could go deep inside himself, and he often did.

On his parents' death he had wandered for days, asking for wisdom to guide his people, asking for knowledge.

He had been here last year, when his mind had been black, though before the tragedy of his parents' end.

Returning from Aristo, from the coronation of Queen Stefania, he had come here for peace. He had not deliberately ignored Layla that day; he had actually hoped to speak a few words to her, to find out a little about the woman he would inevitably marry. But the coronation had brought up strange feelings, but not memories, for he could picture nothing.

Feelings Xavian had known it would be safer to ignore—and he had tried.

He had flown to Europe, had partied, had played the part of playboy prince with zeal, yet nothing had quietened his rising unrest.

And now, as Xavian sat alone in the desert, he found himself hoping for silence, for his racing mind to still—except the roar of the wind through the canyons seemed to be calling for him to listen, and the golden sands seemed to be shifting, tossing him as if on the ocean… He could hear a child's laughter. It must surely be the wind, but there was no mistaking the playful shrieking. Sitting still in the desert, he could taste a rare freedom—glimpse it, touch it—and he couldn't blame it on dreams this time, because his eyes were wide open.

Layla had soothed him, but she had unsettled him too.

She had brought something familiar to his soul—something he could not place, something that made him question everything now.

He would allow no more questions.

He lay back and stared at the blue sky...
His eyes closed against the bright sun and as
his hand slid from his taut, flat stomach,
instead of meeting sand, it met water and his
fingers dipped into the cold of the ocean. This
propelled him to sit upright, and as he stared
at his dry hand, expecting to see droplets, he
knew that it was happening again, that the
madness was creeping in closer...

This was Qusay's ruler?

He didn't want to be mad, and he didn't
want to think, and neither did he want to
listen—because he was scared he might now
get answers.

As darkness fell the emerging night sky
led him back to the different escape of his
desert tent and his new bride.

The tent was softly lit as he entered. The
ghastly *qanoon* struck up the moment he set
foot inside. The candles flickered and the
table was laid, but Layla was not there
waiting.

'The Queen was tired,' a nervous servant
explained. Nervous because a good wife
would have waited up for him. 'She has
retired for the night.'

Xavian wasn't hungry now, and he wasn't tired either.

Restless with energy, he walked into the sleeping chamber and saw that she was feigning sleep.

'I know you are awake.'

Her eyes remained closed but she shrugged. 'Then you should know that I pretend to be asleep because I don't wish to speak with you.'

At close to midnight, her honesty brought a rare half-laugh from Xavian, and only then did she open her eyes to him.

'It is late,' Layla pointed out. 'You are wise enough to know the desert is dangerous at night…'

'I am used to the desert.'

'Not at night, with no supplies, out alone…'

He *was* alone.

With this he was alone.

Xavian turned off the lamp and climbed into bed beside her, but even as the music stopped still his mind would not rest. He had spoken with the palace doctor recently, and it had taken courage to do so. He had told him his fears and the doctor had warned him not to discuss it with anyone—told him that a feeling of *déjà vu* was sometimes a mild form of seizure. He had given him pills, small pills, that Xavian had accepted but silently refused to take.

He did not trust the doctor.

Ah, but wasn't paranoia another sign of insanity?

He rolled onto his side and tried to close his eyes.

And he could not trust Akmal—how could he tell that pompous little man that at times he, the King, had doubts as to the state of his own mind?

'Xavian?' Bolder in the dark, relieved that he was home, wanting the row to end, Layla did not wait for an invitation. Her hands reached for him, her body coiling around his, but he halted her hand with his wrist, pushed her away and then lay tense and angry in the dark as he felt her confusion beside him.

He closed his eyes, willed sleep, but every time he drifted off he felt again as if he were on water, lying in the middle of the desert… He felt the rise and fall of the ocean beneath him, felt the sun scorching his body. There was nowhere to go for Xavian—and no mistress chambers to send her to here.

Here in the desert, no matter how he

fought it, he was steadily going insane—and there was nothing he could do. Fear, a fear he had never known before nor would ever admit to, meant that it was he that reached for her now, because she was soft and warm, breathing and real and alive.

'Xavian, what is wrong…?' He heard the question in her voice, but he couldn't answer, because he didn't know, so he crushed her questions with his lips.

Layla had been scared when he had been out so long, scared when he had returned in this black mood, nervous and unsure when he had climbed into bed beside her, and shamed when he had rejected her. But now, when he covered her, when his mouth crushed her so hard she could not breathe, there was no fear, no trepidation. She felt it again—felt a different facet of what she had so recently discovered.

Her body, and the delicious flare of them together.

She was confused, but she wasn't scared— she knew at some level that this man, her husband, needed what she could now give him.

He was pushing up her nightdress, her face

was swathed in muslin, and her arms were lifting as he discarded it.

He tasted of salt and desert, so potently male. Unshaven, his rough mouth sought hers, his knees pushing her thighs apart. But she fought him. Not his body, but his speed—because she needed escape too. She rolled his body till she was on top, her thighs straddling him, and Xavian was not impressed.

He wanted escape. He had sought her, and now this…

Prolonged lovemaking he did not need tonight… Maybe later, but not now…

Except she was kissing his sulking mouth, and then down his chest, licking at his dark nipples and biting his flesh, tasting his unwashed skin, and all the while he felt her, tight and tender around his centre… He could feel her soft breasts brushing on his skin and he wanted to touch them, pushed her back so that he could…

And for Layla it was a revelation that she could be so bold—deny him, almost, and yet prolong the moment too. Because he was touching her now, touching her breasts with one hand, and stroking her *there* with the other.

She lost her rhythm, but he held her hips,

guided her to his tip and then pulled her hard down his long length. And he did it again and again, till she was the one who was urgent. She was crying his name as he joined her, as wave upon wave hit, and he pressed deep into her until she was limp, then pulled her into his arms beside him.

He lay in the dark, with the wind howling around—a shrieking desert wind that dragged the sane from their beds in search of its call—and there was no desire to investigate. Nothing Xavian wanted at this moment but this—no questions, no confusion…

He could almost ask her.

He could smell the sweet oils of her body, could feel her soft breast heavy in his hand, hear her deep, regular breathing…and maybe he had his wish, his answer.

With her beside him each night maybe sleep would come more easily, because somehow she let him rest, let him dream. And then he heard his own voice.

'Why would they tether me with rope?'

There was a long silence, and he knew she couldn't answer, but she lifted his hand and he felt the cool of her lips press into the angry wound. Then he heard his voice again.

'I'm starting to remember.'

He felt her pause, and then heard her question. 'Remember what?'

'I don't know.'

All she knew was that this was vital, that this demanded her full attention—which, as Queen, she was used to giving. So she sat up in bed and turned on the lamp. As light flooded the room she watched his expression shutter and realised how foolish she had just been—because she had acted as she would for duty, not as a wife, and certainly not as a lover. She should have lain in the dark and held his hand but it was too late for that now.

'What are you starting to remember?'

'Leave it.' He rolled on his side, and this time it wasn't a gesture of trust nor a compliment.

'Xavian?'

'Go to sleep.'

And it was at that moment Layla realised she had lost him.

# CHAPTER SIX

GLIMPSING the palace from the helicopter, Layla caught her breath. In the late morning sun it glowed like a jewel. The shells and semi-precious stones set in the palace walls all caught the light, and it shimmered on the edge of the desert like an oasis.

She had seen it on her arrival, proud and tall, set on the headland, but had been too nervous about the wedding to take it all in. Now, as they came in from the desert rather than over the ocean, it looked different—*everything* was different. A married woman now, she no longer needed to be veiled, but it was more than that. The man beside her had not only awoken her sexuality but had given her something else, something unexpected, for she loved him.

As closed and as guarded as he was, she loved him.

'It is beautiful….' Layla said to the man who sat beside her, staring broodingly ahead.

But Xavian just shrugged.

She wasn't at all sure that Xavian even wanted her love. She had never had a relationship and had no touchstone, no marker to guide her. Their lovemaking was wonderful—she had woken only this morning to Xavian spooned in behind her, had been deep in the forest of orgasm before she had opened her eyes—but even by the time they had bathed and dressed she had felt his detachment. The man who sat beside her now was just so far removed from the man she was sure she had glimpsed. He was more than a closed book, he was a full library's worth, and if she lived for ever there would still be parts unread.

Over and over she rued the decision she'd made to flood the room with light that night, because now he had plunged her into the dark.

Oh, they spoke, but about nothing— nothing that was important, anyway. She corrected herself. They did speak about important things, like palaces and kingdoms, it was just that these things suddenly had no importance to her any more.

Her eyes flicked to Baja, who clearly saw nothing amiss with Xavian's detached demeanour. Baja had told her to neither expect nor want more, but still Layla did.

Though Xavian took her beyond her wildest dreams at night, Layla was greedy—not just for his body, but for the company of his mind. There had been no harsh words since that night, but every day since, Xavian had risen before sunrise and gone out into the desert, coming home long after dark. The closeness, the sharing that had started to emerge, had been abruptly withdrawn. Each morning when she awoke, emotionally he was gone.

'People are already here!'

Even from the sky, Layla saw the palace was a hive of activity. She could see the private jets and helicopters that told her some of the royals and dignitaries had already arrived for tomorrow's reception, but the bride and groom would not have to meet with them until the formal function and Layla was rather relieved. A week away and she hadn't even turned on her computer, or spoken with her aides, and there would surely be plenty to do!

'I wish my sisters were arriving today…'

Her eyes scanned the jets, trying to make out the crests as they drew closer, but Xavian showed no interest in joining her in this game.

On landing, to save their grand entrance for tomorrow, they were taken to the senior royal wing of the palace that was off-limits to guests, and Xavian showed her dutifully around—from lush gardens to secret doors and passages and the sleeping chamber where, when Layla was in Qusay, they would rest together. It was stunning—the bed so huge and so exquisitely furnished that it should have taken centre stage, but it was a sunken bath by the French doors that caught the eye.

'You can bathe and look out to the ocean if you so desire,' Xavian said, opening the doors to reveal the beach in all its glory. Then he saw her aghast face. 'No one can see you.'

'What if someone is walking on the beach?' Layla checked, walking out onto the balcony with him.

'This cove is for our use only,' Xavian explained. 'These stairs are the only access. There is another stretch of beach that is exclusive to the palace, but this is just for us.'

It really was beautiful. The stunning design assured complete privacy—their whole wing was angled so that no one could glimpse them. Even the air and sea traffic, Xavian explained, was routed to avoid this section of the palace.

'Though for now….' Xavian started, just as Layla spoke too.

'I am afraid that I need to…' She gave a tense smile as they spoke together. She hated the new awkwardness between them, and nodded for Xavian to go first.

'I need to do some work. Hopefully it will not take long, but after a week away…'

'I was about to say the same thing,' Layla admitted. 'There will be much for me to attend to.' She rolled her eyes. 'There will have been a lot of activity while I was away.'

'Activity?' Xavian frowned.

'It does not matter.'

It was back to business and she knew it—not just in work, but in their marriage too.

'I will have an office prepared for you.'

'It should already be arranged,' Layla said, 'I asked my staff to ensure there was one ready for my return.'

There was.

Xavian's large office had a smaller room that adjoined it, one where his PA could work and easily be summoned, but the PA had been temporarily relocated, and the room had been prepared for Layla, following her strict specifications. Her computer was already set up, and a mountain of paperwork waited to greet her, but there was fresh orange blossom in the vases and a jug of sparkling iced water on the table. After Layla walked in she immediately opened the doors to the gardens, but there was a strong breeze, and the ocean was whipping up, so she quickly decided to close them.

'It is rather small,' she pointed out, because even if she loved him she was still Queen, and on that score she refused to make do.

'I will have something more suitable arranged for the next time you are in residence,' Xavian responded. 'I think my staff have done rather well for such short notice.'

'You've had years of notice…' Layla responded crisply. 'You and your aides all knew you would be marrying a working queen…'

Xavian sucked in one of his cheeks and stopped himself from biting on his gum. He was not used to being reprimanded. 'I suppose there is a fully equipped, vast office just waiting for me back in Haydar, for when I am in residence…?' he replied, with more than a dash of sarcasm.

'Of course there is,' Layla said, smirking just a touch, enjoying the purse of his lips at her answer. 'You use a different computer system from myself, but it has been installed for you, and there is paper and envelopes bearing the Royal Qusay Crest, and a seal with your name…'

'I get the picture.' Xavian said. 'Okay—yes, this is a bit small, but for the moment you can work in mine, alongside—'

'No, thank you—though I will leave the adjoining door open, if that is okay with you?'

'We can wave to each other…' Xavian made a thin joke, but Layla had other ideas.

'I won't have time for waving, Xavian. I would like to get through my work as quickly as possible. We have the formal reception tomorrow; there is much to do.'

Which told him—again!

Not that he had time to dwell on it. After the week he had been away, there were a thousand signatures required. But he was looking forward to losing himself in work, to forgetting about guests' arrivals and the reception tomorrow, instead focusing on what he did best: ruling his kingdom.

Akmal, having read through the documents, told Xavian the relevant information and awaited his response as other staff trooped in and out. It was a hive of activity—whereas he noticed a couple of hours later, as he drank coffee, that she had refused, obviously preferring to sip at her water rather than take a break with him, Layla worked completely alone.

He didn't get it.

She had brought an entire entourage with her to Qusay—elders, advisors, her maidens, Baja—yet she sought no one's assistance. He sat watching, liking the tap, tap as she worked on the computer, or the occasional scratch of her pen as she signed off on something or scored a bold line through a page, and he liked the look of deep concentration on her face as she pored over a document.

He could not take his eyes off her.

They had completely different working styles. Layla hardly moved, worked silently on, whereas Xavian worked in short, rapid bursts, pacing his office in between, his restless mind working things out. He paused now, watched a helicopter hover for a short time before landing. His lips were dry.

Work was no longer a sufficient distraction.

Soon… He could feel it. Soon *they* would be here.

He stared at where she sat, but Layla did not look up, so Xavian walked over.

'May I make a suggestion?' So deep in her work was she, Layla hadn't heard him come over, and now he sat on the edge of her desk, looking down at her…

'Please do,' Layla responded, politely but coolly.

'I always have Akmal, or one of my other senior aides, read through things—they highlight the relevant parts. Of course I would prefer to take the time to go through everything personally, but…' He looked at the document she was holding. 'May I?'

His shrewd eyes scanned it in a matter of minutes. 'Here Akmal would have highlighted the fact that I have already approved the drilling to commence for the new sapphire mine…' he skimmed the page again

'…and here is the date that you approved for the opening of the new mine to fund the hospital and pay for doctors…' He was quite enjoying himself, showing her, helping her see just how much time she was wasting, how doing it the hard way wasn't always necessary—and anyway, he wanted to take her upstairs and go to bed.

Actually, ruling was what he did second best!

'There is nothing new in this document; it just requires your signature.'

'No,' Layla said very deliberately, very slowly. 'I approved the drilling for a new *opal* mine—the income from that mine was to fund a teaching hospital…for Haydar to begin the process of educating doctors instead of importing them.'

'I see.'

'No, Xavian, you don't. Your elders and advisors listen to you—I have heard you this morning, giving orders and expecting them to be followed.'

'Of course.'

'My country resists change. It is my opinion that we have relied on the sapphire mines to support us for too long. Yes, we are wealthy, but we are far from self-suffcent. I shop in Aristo for my clothes; we send our most promising children overseas for higher education. Yes, we have the best doctors, because we rely on the mines to fund them… What happens if the mines do not yield?'

'They are plentiful, though.'

'Or if a vast sapphire mine is discovered here in Qusay?' Layla offered. 'We have other exports, of course, but I would like to see Haydar truly flourish and prosper, to be truly self-sufficient—and yet my advisors and elders resist.' She ran a tired hand over her brow. 'At every turn they change things, little details that they hope I will not notice…'

'Fire them.'

'I cannot. To appease the people when he did not produce a son, my father passed long and complicated legislation. The elders have considerable weight.'

'But you are Queen,' Xavian, said. 'Ultimately you rule.'

'Of course,' Layla responded. 'Which is why I check everything, and which is why—' she gave a short smile that didn't even turn her lips '—I will sit for several more hours, reading paperwork that they hope I am too tired for.'

She lowered her head and tried to continue reading. He knew he should leave her to work—on any other day he would have—except helicopters were still landing outside, and soon *they* would be here. He would far rather be here with her than alone with his thoughts, Xavian decided, playing with a strand of her hair.

'Leave it for now, Layla.'

'I cannot,' Layla said, biting her lip as his hand slipped under her hair and now stroked the back of her neck. 'In time, as you slowly come to understand the ways of Haydar…' He stood now, and still she did not look up. The words she *had* to read blurred on the page as he lifted her hair. She felt his lips on the back of her neck and *how* she wanted to turn to him, to ask for his help, to trust him with her burden. But she had trusted once before: Noor's husband, Ahmed, her own brother-in-law. A prince himself, he had shouldered some of the burden, till the elders had worked their ways on him too, reminding him of his guilty secret and the shame it would cause if it got out. But Ahmed was weak, Layla reminded herself, whereas Xavian was strong.

His warm lips nuzzled her neck, and how she wanted to leave the paperwork, to be with him—to be a wife.

'Just leave it for now, Layla, surely it can wait…?'

And she glimpsed it then—the impossibility of it all. Xavian's first duty was to Qusay—or right now his first duty was satisfying his ardour. What did he care if she signed away a hard fought-for hospital so long as he got his way?

'Surely *you* can wait?'

'Tonight we have to sleep apart…'

Xavian reminded her of the annoying custom that, even though they were married, on the night before the formal reception she was to be readied as if a new bride. His hands were on her breasts now as still he kissed her neck, stroking them, cupping them through the fabric. She could feel her panties damp…she wanted to rest back against his body…except she could not, must not give in and rest awhile in his arms—duty had to come first.

'I am trying to work, Xavian!' Her voice

came out too brittle, and she jerked her body away too sharply, but it was either that or succumb.

'Then work,' Xavian said tartly, and as he left her alone with her precious documents he was not best pleased. He was not used to strong women, nor to women who refused his advances.

He walked over to the window and silently fumed, seeing but not focusing on the arriving guests. The thick glass silenced the buzz of the helicopter rotors, the noise of royals and their aides spilling out on the manicured lawn... But then his mind stopped thinking about work, and about a wife who sometimes did not act like one—his blood turned to ice as Queen Stefania stepped out... How she had changed. Gone were the frumpy creations she had worn in the early days of her marriage to King Zakari—now, even having just had a baby, she was sleek and well groomed. But it was only a passing glance he gave her... His eyes were fixed on the helicopter door, and he could feel the sweat beading on his forehead, his hands bunched into fists as he waited. Then suddenly there he was.

King Zakari Al'Farisi, dressed in a pale blue robe, strode across the lawn and caught up with his wife. She must have said something that pleased him, because he smiled and then looked up at the palace, looked straight up to the window where Xavian stood. Though he knew it was impossible, knew no one could see in, Xavian stepped back. He knew they would soon be inside the palace now, and his breath was coming rapidly through his nostrils because his jaw was clamped together. The dread that had been chasing him, swirling around him for so long, had captured him now, enclosing him… And then he turned and saw Layla, oblivious, calm, and he wanted her in a different way.

'Layla!'

She glanced up and he saw her frown. He wanted her to come over to the window, to show her, to tell her—and then there was a knock at the door and Akmal came in. Xavian felt as if he lived in a goldfish bowl at times—a vast, luxurious one, perhaps, but a goldfish bowl all the same.

'Wait till I tell you to enter!' Xavian snapped, and Layla felt her cheeks pinken at how embarrassing it might have been had Akmal walked in just a few minutes earlier—or, worse, if she had given in to her own secret wishes and Xavian's demands.

'I apologise, Sire, but I wanted to inform you that King Zakari of Calista and Queen Stefania of Aristo have arrived.'

'We are expecting many guests,' Xavian answered evenly, but there was something in his voice that had Layla's eyes snap to him. She could see a muscle leaping in his cheek as he continued, 'I do not need to be informed when people arrive—it is customary that we greet them tomorrow, at the formal reception.'

'They have asked if they may dine with you tonight,' Akmal went on boldly. 'Of course it is irregular, but these *are* the rulers of the Kingdom of Adamas.'

'No.' He gave no elaboration, no qualification, just a straight no.

'Perhaps I could suggest that you meet for refreshments this afternoon? Only they have to fly back to Calista straight after the reception. They have asked that I explain that their son, Prince Zafir, is too young to be left for long.'

'No.' Again Xavian's response was direct,

and he dismissed a worried-looking Akmal, who now somehow had to soften his King's rude refusal.

'It might be nice to dine with them…' Layla suggested once they were alone. She knew better than to argue in front of Akmal. 'Or just to spend a little time with them. Perhaps they can offer us some advice—after all, they too rule two separate lands…'

'I have given my answer.'

'The invitation extends to both of us.' Layla would not be silenced. 'I would love to accept.'

'You will follow my wishes,' Xavian retorted sharply. 'In my palace, in my home, you will follow my rules.'

'I follow my own rules, Xavian.' She stood defiant before him. 'Don't try and pull rank on me just to get your way. There is surely time at least to take refreshments with them?'

'I thought you said that you *had* to work,' Xavian retorted. 'You made it clear that you are too busy to spend time with me, to satisfy me, and yet you are happy to make small talk with strangers.'

'Satisfy you!' She bristled at his choice of words. 'Is that what I'm here for?'

'We are supposed to be producing an heir…' Xavian said nastily. 'I am sure your people would rather you concentrated on getting pregnant than worried about some hospital or how Haydar will spend its billions.' She was too stunned to deliver a response, so, savagely he continued. 'I suggest that you need to sort out your priorities, Layla—because, frankly, they're shot!'

And with that he stalked out. Layla blinked as he slammed the heavy door behind him. She had no idea what had just happened—there was no warning of these black moods; they just swept in from nowhere—yet she refused to run after him, even if it meant she wouldn't see him now till the reception.

She sat down and picked up her documents, willing herself to concentrate even though her hands were shaking, even though her heart was hammering. But she couldn't. Putting down the documents, she rested her head in her hands. Oh, his words had stung, and she was a long way from trusting him with her burdens, but there was something else that knotted her stomach, something else that had fingers of dread squeezing around her heart.

There was something seriously wrong. She knew it.

She closed her eyes, cast her mind back to the last time Xavian had been like this, when he had suddenly chosen to go deep into the desert... They had been in the bath—talking, bathing, laughing, loving, sharing...

And then she looked up—looked up unseeing, blinking a couple of times. She had been talking about the coronation, the night she had stood beside him and he hadn't even known she was there, talking about Queen Stefania and King Zakari that time too.

But it made no sense—how could rulers from another land, people he barely knew, affect him so?

## CHAPTER SEVEN

HE HAD dreaded this day.

Xavian did not wake, because he had not slept. He had been tempted, on so many levels, to break with tradition and join Layla—had even walked down the corridor. But Baja had sat outside the bedroom, guarding the Queen, assuring that she rested, and her currant eyes had held his for a long, silent moment before Xavian had retreated.

For months Xavian had dreaded this—not his wedding, but the reception.

Since the Aristan coronation, in fact. Lining up at the Aristan palace, waiting to greet the newly crowned Queen, he had had little idea of what awaited him.

There had been moments prior to that, of course. Sometimes over the years he would turn the wrong way in a corridor and there would be a small flash of confusion, when the door he was expecting wasn't there and then, there had always been the dreams.

Dreams that even as a child had troubled him, though they were not nightmares. Xavian had never ridden a horse, yet in his dreams he did—could feel the powerful movement of the beast, could hear his brothers laughing.

He was dreaming of what he yearned for, his mother had explained, for the brothers she could not give him and the horses that she forbade.

And it *had* made sense.

Till the coronation.

Glancing down the line-up, he had felt his eyes drawn to King Zakari—to a face that somehow he knew well—and he had felt dread rising. Then he had realised he was not alone with this feeling, because as the Queen had greeted him Xavian had seen the shock on Stefania's face, the question in her eyes as they met his. Such shock that she had paled and almost fainted. Zakari had stepped in then, had swept her away without even a glance towards Xavian.

It should have been forgotten.

But then the letters had started.

And telephone calls too.

Sometimes an invitation.

All of them he had ignored—yet now duty gave him no choice but to face them.

Xavian was usually happiest when alone and pensive, but today he didn't want to think—he had even inspected the ballroom where the function would take place, just to fill his time. Today he could not stand to be alone. This day would be impossible without Layla there with him.

Usually he gave no thought to a row, but he felt a rare need to put things right, to have her by his side today for reasons other than duty.

Until Layla he had known nothing of true need—all his desires, be they thirst, women or power, were instantly met—yet with Layla there was no ending. The need remained. A different need—an endless need—and one he could not explain.

Once shaven and bathed, and with too many hours till he saw Layla again, Xavian's patience ran out as Akmal came in to go through the finer details.

'Here is the Qusay emerald necklace.' He

opened the box for Xavian's sighting. 'The Queen will wear this tonight.'

Xavian looked at the glittering jewels that were to be worn by the wife of the Qusay King at all official functions. It was a clear show of wealth, the finest stones had been cut and polished to display the best of Qusay, and surely he should be the one to give it to her?

'I will give it to Layla myself.'

'She is to wear it this evening, though.' Akmal pointed out. 'She is being prepared...'

'Then I will take it to her now.'

His eyes dared Akmal to argue. He was tired of tradition, Xavian told himself as he summoned his dresser and put on the royal wedding robes—it was a stupid tradition anyway, he decided, as his *kafeya* was secured with thick gold braid. They were already husband and wife; why should they be kept apart? He was King, he made the rules, and surely, he thought, as he walked through the corridors to her door, it was a *better* tradition that he, the ruler, presented her with this gift.

All this he told himself as he pushed open the door, not quite prepared to admit yet that the only person he wanted to see now, the one person he needed to get through this day, was her.

# CHAPTER EIGHT

SHE sat in the milky waters, her skin soft, soaking in the oils and fragrances, her black hair piled on her head, gazing out of the opened balcony doors to the dreamy ocean. Her maidens were laying out her dress, everything was in place, and yet she could not relax.

There had been numerous functions in her life, too many to count or remember, and she knew well the loneliness of sitting at elaborate meals with an aide at her side. Tonight, though, she would be with Xavian, tonight she would have her husband at her side—and yet still she felt lonely

He made her lonely.

He had made no attempt to apologise. It was not his place to say sorry, Xavian would no doubt remind her, if she pushed for an apology.

He had promised to provide—which he did.

He had promised to give her an heir—which he surely would…perhaps already had.

Her hand moved to her stomach and she wondered as to the miracle that might already be taking place.

She should be content, but she wasn't.

Layla almost wished that Baja had been right—that their mating had been clinical, just another duty to perform—but it was so much more…and still she wanted more from him. Wanted not just an *heir*, but *their* child—wanted a husband not just in name.

And then he walked in, and her confused, troubled eyes turned to him, and she just lay there in the bath in silence as he dismissed her staff and closed the door.

Never had he looked more beautiful

Cleanshaven for the first time since the desert, he was dressed in black robes edged with gold. He looked powerful, commanding, and utterly breathtaking—but she was too proud and too angry to just demur.

'You are not supposed to be here.'

'It's a stupid rule.'

'For you, perhaps,' Layla said, 'but I rather

like it. It is nice to have peace—nice to rest and prepare for such an occasion.'

'It is stupid that we slept alone…'

'There will be many nights together soon…' Layla shrugged, the water rippling around her, and all Xavian wanted to do was climb in and to kiss her sulking mouth.

'You did not miss me last night?' Xavian said. 'You did not lie awake thinking of me?'

'Of course I did,' Layla said. 'I was so angry I lay awake wishing I could give you a piece of my mind, deliver the perfect retort to your crass words… It was, I will admit, rather frustrating.'

And even on this day, even as dread clutched his heart, as unknown fears took vivid shape, still she made him smile.

She was his match.

His dark eyes roamed her creamy shoulders, and if want could part waters then she would lie bare for his approval. He sat on the edge of the bath without a word, just watching her, and then he held out the gift for his Queen.

She had her choice of jewels, had worn so many beautiful pieces that jewellery sometimes bored her—but not this. The cascading necklace of emeralds and diamonds made her eyes widen because it was a masterpiece, its jewels fell from each other like an emerald fountain, but it wasn't sufficient.

'Is this how you apologise?' He heard the tart edge of resistance in her voice.

'It would seem not.'

'Jewellery will not placate me.'

'I am sorry for the things that I said.' He had never said those words, and she had never expected to hear them from him. She had been prepared for an explanation, perhaps a hint of reason, but never the words 'I am sorry', and they caught her completely off-guard. They confused her too, because he had given her just a little bit more of himself and surely, because this was Xavian, he would take it away again soon. 'There is much on my mind.'

'Like what?' she challenged.

Xavian shook his head.

'You won't tell me?'

'Have you told *me* everything, Layla?' Xavian asked, watching her cheeks pinken. 'Have you told me all that is on your mind?'

'No.'

'Why?'

The silence was endless, and it was Xavian who broke it.

'One day we will,' Xavian said, and her heart soared at the possibility, 'One day, I hope soon, we will be ready to share—but not on this day. There are things we have to get through, things that need to be done. I ask you to forgive me for yesterday, to accept I have things on my mind and to know I hope for different things for us. You are more than a wife to me, Layla.'

'You are more than a husband to me,' Layla admitted. 'And I accept both your apology and your gift.'

'The apology is from me,' Xavian said. 'The gift is from the rich land. This necklace was worn by my mother and my grandmother, and many before them—for generations the King's bride has worn this…' His voice was as mesmerising as the jewels that he took from the box. 'The finest stones mined from the heart of Qusay have been cut and fashioned. This necklace reminds our people of our riches…of the land that keeps us well nourished with its rare gifts.'

He leant forward and draped the necklace across her chest. She could feel the cool weight of the stones on her skin and then he moved behind her, connecting the clasp and letting the necklace drop.

'Tonight you wear the Qusay necklace; tonight our people will see the beauty of this union…'

He was proud of her, he was telling her that, and it was the closest she had come to his love.

'We will work out a way…' From behind he kissed her bare shoulder slowly, deeply. She felt the weight of his mouth and then the bliss of his words. 'When this day is over we will move forward—we will work out a way that we can be together properly…' His warm hands were soaping her breasts. She wanted to lean back into him, to drag him in to join her, and the knowledge that she couldn't teased her senses. He was dressed in his finery, and she squirmed naked beneath him as his mouth worked her shoulders, as his hands worked her tender breasts. She was dizzy with lust, breathless at the thought of their new future. On and on he kissed her, and with just his mouth on her neck, his words in her ears and his hands on her breasts she was in a frenzy. She could feel the tiny beats of her pulse beneath the water that pleaded for him to join her, that left her aroused and yearning for more, and then wickedly he stood and smiled down at her.

'You can't leave me like this…'

'I am saving you for later—it will be our reward when this night is over.'

He stared down at her beauty—at the hair that would be in his fingers tonight, at the jewels around her throat, at her ripe breasts—and knew she was his and all was right. He stared out to the ocean, feeling so strong now from just seeing her that he could surely hold it back if he chose to.

'What do you do to me, Layla?'

She did not know, but he did it to her too. He made her bold and alive and wanton, and she reached out and felt him, hard beneath her fingers, and she loved the game, loved the chase, loved the want in him too.

'You will find out later.'

Her body thrummed with the promise of *later* even after he was gone. Baja was talking as she dressed her in a long ivory gown, and the maidens were putting the final touches to her hair—snaky ringlets piled on her head. And despite the beautician's attempts, no make-up could douse the pink flush in her cheeks! Her kohl-rimmed violet eyes glittered at the prospect of tonight, of tomorrow, of a *real* life with Xavian.

Slipping on high, beaded shoes, she was ready at last, and it was exciting to see her reflection, to anticipate the appreciation in Xavian's eyes. The necklace really was stunning, and teardrop emerald earrings were the final touch. It was time for them to be presented to the world as a couple. She felt as if her heart would explode in joy—because never had she dreamed of this.

Akmal announced her King's arrival, and Baja and the handmaidens faded into the distance as he stepped into the chamber.

She saw him swallow, and then a slow, rare smile lightened his chiselled features.

'You look wonderful.'

'So do you!' Layla said. 'And I have a gift for you.' She handed him a ring. 'It is a rare sapphire from Haydar…'

'It matches your eyes…' Xavian said as he looked at the deep violet-blue stone.

'I notice you do not wear jewellery.' Layla swallowed. As King he would have plenty to choose from, yet Xavian wore none. 'If you prefer not to wear it you can keep it upon your person…'

'I will wear it with pride.' He admired the stone. 'Was this worn by your father?'

'Our traditions are different, Xavian. The gift you gave is from your land, your country, whereas this gift is from me. You are right—it was chosen as it matches your bride's eyes, but, no, it shall not be passed down…' He stared at the ring that he held near his finger. 'You take this to your grave.'

So many times his dressers had given him trinkets, pieces that carried the royal crest, yet none had ever felt right. This ring did.

He offered her his arm and she took it.

As they walked through the long corridors of the palace, past portraits and ancient Bedouin hangings, through rooms full of history as they began to make their own, she was suddenly nervous.

It was a significant moment in time: Qusay and Haydar would by united; two rulers would merge.

She heard the chatter behind the ballroom door hush as the royal couple's arrival was announced and she caught Xavian's eye.

'Nervous?'

'Of course not…' Layla lied—because that was her number one rule: never let anyone fully in, never let anyone know the weight of her burden, the strain. And yet, soon…soon she would share with Xavian, during the glorious month that lay ahead. She glimpsed their sharing, glimpsed a future not just with a husband, but with a partner, and a slow warmth flooded her. It wrapped around her like a safety blanket and comforted her as the heavy doors opened and a long line of people stood in resplendent, regal glory. Every eye turned to them, and saw for the first time the Queen who had been hidden behind a veil,

'Your Royal Highnesses, dignitaries, distinguished guests… Please welcome the bride and groom—King Xavian of Qusay and Queen Layla of Haydar. I present to you the King and Queen of Qusay and Haydar.'

# CHAPTER NINE

THERE was an unnerving amount of royals and dignitaries to meet, but by other royal standards it was small.

First the immediate successors to Xavian, until Layla produced an heir, were introduced.

'Sheikh Prince Kareef of Qais,' Akmal announced, and Kareef bowed and then spoke with Xavian before smiling to Layla. 'It is an honour to be here.'

Layla smiled and returned the greeting, but she was mesmerised by his eyes—they were the same blue as in the portraits that lined the walls of the palace, and he was dressed in the same black and gold as Xavian. It dawned on her then that she was meeting her new family, and Xavian must have understood that too, because he broke with tradition and added just a little more information than Akmal's formalities allowed. 'My cousins,' he said. 'I have told Layla many tales…'

And that alone made her heart soar, because Xavian was telling his family, letting them know before her very eyes, that this was more than a marriage of duty.

'Sheikh Rafiq of Qusay…' Akmal moved them on and she was greeted by a very different cousin—his eyes were blue, like his brother's, but—as Xavian had explained when first they had become close—in slight rebellion Rafiq was dressed in Western clothes. He was immaculate, arrogant, confident, yet somehow, from his smile, she knew he was really rather nice. Xavian's family were certainly interesting…

'Is Tahir here?' Xavian asked.

There was a slight pause, before Kareef smoothly answered. 'He was unable to get away. He sends his apologies and of course offers you both his best wishes for your future happiness…'

Xavian knew it had been improper to ask, that Tahir's absence should not have been commented on, but he was genuinely curious. Xavian's youngest cousin was his favourite, but he had left Qusay years ago and never returned. Xavian still missed him, wondered about him, even worried for him a little. There was no time to dwell, however. The row was long and all Xavian wanted was it to be over—not that anyone could tell, for he spoke easily with the guests, met Layla's many sisters and their husbands. But occasionally, despite willing himself not to, he let his eyes drift beyond, to a couple whose eyes were fixed on him. And how he wanted to turn, to walk out, to ignore—but, as always, duty, protocol, dictated otherwise.

Layla was floating on a cloud, simply glowing, but as the family introductions were over she felt a shift in Xavian, a tension building as they walked down the line, and she did not understand it even when she faced it.

'Sheikh King Zakari and Sheikha Queen Stefania from the Kingdom of Adamas.'

'Your Highness…' Layla's smile wavered as she greeted Sheikha Queen Stefania, for the Queen of Aristo was not looking at her. Instead her eyes were on Xavian as he greeted her husband, and then Stefania seemed to remember her place.

'Queen Layla…' She curtsied deeply. 'We are honoured to be here.'

And then Layla met King Zakari. Offered her hand and stared into eyes that, though his mouth smiled, were filled with deep concern.

'Adamas offers its prayers and best wishes…' His voice was gruff, and she could sense nervousness, but Xavian had moved swiftly on, making quick work of the line. Finally it was over, finally they were being led to their seats, with the room standing until the King and Queen were duly seated.

He was rigid beside her and made no attempt at small talk, just nodded when Akmal came over once and spoke in his ear. Only when the first speeches had been given and the first course of the sumptuous banquet was served did Layla get a chance to speak with Xavian. She wanted to know what was going on—she could feel Zakari watching them.

'Is everything all right?'

'Of course…' Xavian took a long drink of iced water.

'There is something going on.'

'I don't know what you are talking about.'

'King Zakari…'

'Layla…' His voice was brittle, interrupting her question, and she blinked at its harshness. Even Xavian seemed to regret his tone and he took another drink of water before continuing. 'I did not want to trouble you with this, but as you insist on knowing… Just as we entered, Sheikh Rafiq received word that there has been an explosion at a warehouse in New Zealand—some of his workers have been injured.' The horror was evident in her face, but she quickly recovered so as not to upset their guests. 'You will understand that he needed to leave swiftly…'

Her eyes shot to the empty seat beside Kareef…

'So he has gone?'

'Of course. He has to look after his staff… We are honoured that he stayed so long.'

Which should have explained everything, of course.

She glanced over to the table and again caught Queen Stefania's worried glance. This time Layla gave a thin smile back—a smile of acknowledgement, a small, brief nod—letting her know that she knew what the problem was, that Xavian had explained, that she understood…

So why didn't Stefania smile back?

And why did Layla still feel as if she knew nothing?

# CHAPTER TEN

THERE were fine gowns and jewels on display, a feast to be consumed, traditional music to dance to… And yet, despite all the promise of earlier that evening, the night Layla had had such high hopes for seemed to have ended at their entrance. It was business, that was all, another formal function and one not made particularly easy by Xavian, who was wooden and formal by her side.

It was how she had imagined her future to be, just not how she had so recently dreamed it.

Still, it was almost over—protocol dictated that the newlyweds leave first, and Akmal had advised them that it was time. Thankfully there were no long rounds of goodbyes. The room rose as they made their exit, and Layla finally breathed out. So too did

Xavian—at last he seemed to relax, now that it was over.

'Come…' Xavian said. 'Let us go to bed…' How sweet those words sounded, such a wonderful reward for good behaviour, and she let him take her by the hand and lead her to the staircase. The music was still playing but the party was winding down. For this couple hopefully it had just begun.

'Your Highness… King Xavian…' She felt Xavian tense, and realised he was ignoring Akmal as he climbed the stairs. 'Your Highness…' Akmal scurried to the bottom of the stairs. 'I apologise for disturbing you, but King Zakari and Queen Stefania have requested to speak with you.'

'I am going to bed.' Xavian didn't even turn round.

'Your Highness…'

'Did you not hear what I said?' Xavian snapped. 'I have retired for the night.'

He did not want this conversation.

All night he had avoided it.

Avoided them.

He had felt King Zakari's eyes on him, always trying to meet his, and always he had sensed Queen Stefania watching him.

'They have made a formal request.'

Akmal's words should have halted him, but they did not.

Xavian had greeted them without looking at them, had welcomed them, accepted their official congratulations without meeting their eyes, and now, just when he had thought he had dealt with it, just when he'd thought it was over, that they would be returning to Calista, that he could finally *breathe*, Akmal had approached with the request he had been secretly dreading.

'Your Highness.' Akmal was at his most annoying, most insistent. 'They are neighbouring rulers; it is unthinkable that I tell them you have declined this request.'

'My wife is exhausted…'

'I am fine,' Layla clipped, refusing to allow Xavian to speak for her, or use her as an excuse—especially when none was needed. 'Of course we shall meet with them.'

The scars on his wrists often hurt, and now they throbbed. The wounds felt so raw they could be new.

Wounds.

Little rocks were pelting him, he could

feel the sweat on his forehead. He did not want Layla to see him like this.

To hear the news like this.

'I will see them alone.' As Akmal swept off, he turned to Layla. 'Go to bed.' He saw the flash in her eyes at his curt dismissal. 'I may join you...'

'May join me?' Layla frowned.

'I don't know how long this will take,' Xavian snapped. 'I do not want to disturb you. Do not wait up.'

He left her standing there—could offer her no further explanation because he wasn't sure himself what was coming.

He was in dread.

'There is nothing to weep over...' Baja undressed her and put her in a nightrobe... 'Your fertile time is past—maybe you are already with child. It is better your body rests now than serves his needs each night.'

'You don't understand...' Layla sobbed, because she couldn't help it. He had done it again—offered her hope and then taken it back. 'It was not like you said. It was better...it was more than I ever expected...'

'Good...' Baja guided her to the bed. 'I am

glad that he was considerate. But now it is time for you to rest. Do not lose your head, Layla…' Baja knew well the wilful Queen's impetuous ways, knew her passion and her imagination that, left unchecked, could surely only get her into trouble. 'Your mind must be clear for ruling—not lusting…'

'He's my husband.'

'Whose wishes you must honour and respect… without question!' Baja said as Layla opened her mouth to argue. 'Even if you are Queen, in bed—in private—you are his wife.' Baja was the only person who could speak like this with Layla—she was more of a mother than her own mother had been—and even if she did not like what she said, always she spoke wisely, and Layla knew she truly did care.

'He said things would be different, that after the reception things would be different.'

'And again he has proved otherwise,' Baja pointed out.

'I'm confused…' She was just so tired and bewildered from trying to work him out.

'Men do that.' Baja smiled. 'They know what to say, to do, to make our bodies succumb, and that is okay so long as you only lose yourself for a little while. But never, not for a moment, can a Queen lose her head and her heart belongs to her people. Those last words are yours, Layla.'

They had been.

Before she had met Xavain those had been her very words, but things were not so simple now.

'So I cannot love my husband?'

'Of course you can love him—but you must stay safe and remember that he is King first. His heart will be with his people.'

But she wanted it with *her*.

# CHAPTER ELEVEN

HE DID not want this.

Xavian did not want this conversation to happen…

He closed his eyelids, pressed the bridge of his nose between finger and thumb. He was King, he was strong, he could deal with anything—even the truth…

He pulled in air, straightened his shoulders and then left his study. He nodded to Akmal to open the door, but as his vizier walked in behind him Xavian turned.

'Alone.'

Akmal did not have the nerve to argue, he could sense the King's volatile mood, but he felt like a cat put out in the rain. Usually he sat in with international dignitaries, and the King and Queen of Adamas were important people, relations must be forged…and *how* he wanted to know what was going on.

The greetings were semi-formal—hands shaken, seats taken, and a moment or two of polite conversation—and then it was Zakari who cleared his throat. His wife, Queen Stefania, was wringing her hands nervously in her lap.

'We would like to thank you and the people of Qusay for your gift on the birth of our son,' Zakari said.

'You are most welcome,' Xavian responded. Usually he would have little or no idea what gift had been sent, his staff would have taken care of such details, but in this case Xavian had taken more interest. A stunning eighteen-carat emerald had been cut and polished and sent to celebrate the birth. 'How is your son?'

'Zafir is doing well.' Xavian could feel Zakari's eyes on him, and he kept his face impassive, but hearing Zakari say the child's name brought a fresh surge of unease. Almost a confirmation of why he was here. 'Do you know anything of our history?' Zakari asked.

'But of course…' Xavian duly answered. 'Two islands, Aristo and Calista, that have been reunited by your marriage to form the Kingdom of Adamas. That is why it is such a pleasure to speak privately with you—Layla and I have high hopes for Qusay and Haydar's future, and it will be interesting to speak—'

'I was referring to my family history,' Zakari interrupted. 'Do you know much about it?'

'Some.' Xavian's voice was suddenly hoarse, and he poured himself some water.

'My mother died and my father remarried.'

'I see.' Xavian flashed a non-committal smile.

'He brought five sons with him to the marriage. Anya, Queen of Calista, could not have children, so she adopted us...the five sons...'

'I am aware,' Xavian said. 'Perhaps we could discuss how the Calistan people—?'

'When we were boys two of my brothers—the twins, Aarif and Kaliq—built a raft. They were playing a game; they wanted to sail...' Zakari ignored Xavian's attempt to change the subject, his voice just a touch louder, his story clearly well rehearsed. His wife pulled out a handkerchief and Xavian just sat there, staring at the wall beyond the King's shoulder. 'Our youngest brother, Zafir, who was only six at the time, begged to join them on their adventure. They were foolish to allow him to of course, but teenagers often are foolish...'

'Your Highness.' It was Xavian who spoke louder now. 'With all due respect, it is late'

'They were captured by pirates…' Zakari's words were relentless and Xavian stood.

'I must bid you goodnight.'

'Their wrists were bound for two days and nights.' Zakari stood too. 'Zafir managed to get his undone and free his brothers. Aarif was shot in the face as they tried to escape—he fell into the water. Kaliq dived in to save him, but the raft, with Zafir on board, drifted off…'

Xavian refused to be polite now. He walked off, crossed the living room, swinging around angrily when Zakari dared—*dared* to halt him by grabbing at his arm. 'Please listen.'

'I have heard enough…' Xavian was sweating, yet his voice was calm. He was talking kindly, as he would to a mad man who persisted with his delusions. 'My wife is tired; she is waiting for me…'

'Zafir was never seen again. We have searched endlessly…'

'I am sorry for your loss,' Xavian said patiently, but Zakari was not listening. Stefania was crying in the background as he moved to lift the sleeve of Xavian's robe. Xavian's hand halted him. 'I must leave.'

'Please…' Zakari's strong voice broke. 'Please, just listen. At Stefania's coronation you helped my wife when she felt faint. She saw the scars on your wrist, she recognised your eyes—Zafir, *I* recognise you…'

'Enough.' Xavian tried to pull back his wrist, but he couldn't. He was as strong as Zakari, but it wasn't strength that stopped him moving. It was strength that kept his wrist there, strength that anchored him as finally he faced the truth…

'These are the marks on my brothers' wrists…' Zakari's black eyes actually filled with tears as he saw the same thick scars his brothers wore.

'Impossible…' Xavian said, except now there was question in his husky voice. 'How it could be possible?' he asked. 'I could not have just appeared.'

'Xavian…' For the first time Stefania spoke. 'Do you remember when I felt faint at the coronation—you helped me…?'

Xavian nodded. He didn't resist, he didn't persist, he just stood there and faced it.

'It took time to remember, but when it had

all died down I remembered the scars on your wrists, that when looking into your eyes I felt as if I recognised you. You have the eyes of your brothers.'

Xavian had never cried in his life, and determinedly he did not cry now as the Queen spoke on. He just stood there and took it as his world fell apart. As everything he possessed, everything he knew, slipped away.

'I was wary of approaching Zakari. It just did not seem possible that you, ruler of Qusay, were somehow his brother. I did some research—for months I have been reading about your family, about you. I read old newspapers, read how there was only one heir, that the people of Qusay were concerned because he was never seen, that there were rumours he was an ill child.'

'I *was* sick…' Xavian said. 'I had seizures. For my early childhood I was—'

'I found an article, a report that you were believed close to death…that was two days after Zafir went missing. The paper reported that a reputable source inside the palace had said that the people of Qusay were to prepare for bad news…'

'I was a delicate child.'

'The next day the paper recanted. The palace doctor made a speech and said that yes, indeed, the young prince *was* gravely ill, but was in time expected to make a full recovery. In just a few hours a delicate, sickly child, close to death, was suddenly expected to make a full recovery... There are no photos of Xavian as a child, save one official portrait where he is sleeping...'

'No.' He tried to discount it, and now he did resist. 'Too many people would know...' He shook his head. 'No...' He was angry now, angry at his confusion. He wanted this to go away, except it wouldn't.

'Please, I know the distress this must cause you...' Stefania begged.

'You know nothing,' Xavian sneered, wrenching open the door. Akmal practically fell inside, and judging from his pale face he had clearly heard at least some of what had been said.

'Is this true?

'Of course not, Sire. This is preposterous, a lie...' Xavian might not like Akmal very much, but he never doubted that he spoke the truth—and from his outrage he knew that he was not lying now. 'Yes, there was a time when you were gravely ill. I was not as senior then, but I did speak with the elders. The doctor was at your side night and day…and slowly you recovered. It was a miracle, really; you were so sick…'

He stared up at the strong, muscular frame of his King and blinked, over and over, just stood and blinked as his world too started to crumble. 'No…' Of course he denied it, because he just couldn't comprehend it. 'As if they could replace him…' He shook his head at the impossibility. 'No. I was here. I would know…' And then he blinked again, opened his mouth to say something. But there was just an appalled silence for the longest time. And then he got angry. For the first time Akmal was rude to royalty, and he pointed his finger accusingly at the rulers of Adamas. 'Of course it is not true. They lie…they refuse to accept that Zafir is dead…'

'It is true.' Xavian's voice was strong even as everything collapsed beneath him, as he freed the truth that for months, perhaps years, had been trying to escape from his very soul. He stared into his brother's black eyes and recognised his own, and then looked down to the thick scars on his wrists that sometimes seemed to burn him at night. 'Since the coronation I have known something was wrong. My parents did not want me to go. Now I know why.'

'How long have you known the truth?' Zakari asked, tears in his eyes for his brother's pain.

'About five minutes,' Xavian admitted. 'But it has been growing inside for a while. I thought I was going insane. I could hear children laughing… I can remember chasing a bird in the palace…'

For the first time Zakari almost smiled.

'I remember that too.'

'My mother?' That face he had recognised in his dreams flashed before him, and he would have given up all he had with ease just to see her. 'Anya—my stepmother…?'

'She died.' Zakari's face was pale, because only now was he glimpsing his brother's horror. For years he had searched, had prayed, had dreamt of this reunion, but he had never envisaged this pain. 'Our father too.'

Xavian was angry, and Akmal was the closest. 'Of *course* you knew—you *all* knew…'

'No!' he pleaded. 'I was not vizier then…

I would never lie to you.' And then Akmal broke down and his own truth emerged. 'I did question things many years back—but I was silenced, Sire…' He wept. 'One night we were sure we had lost you…' He corrected himself then, as Xavian closed his eyes. 'Or rather that we had lost Prince Xavian. But the next day the doctor said you still clung to life. A few weeks later I saw the Queen, walking with you in the gardens. You were still weak, in a chair…' Akmal wept at the memory that had at the time cheered him so. 'It was the first time I had seen you in years. Always you were shut away, and to see you, awake…'

'Did I talk?'

'No…' Akmal admitted. 'You were silent for a long while, except with your parents… We thought the seizures had damaged your brain, but you got stronger, and you were so clever, but never a happy child…'

Was it any wonder?

'King Xavian,' Akmal pleaded, 'this cannot get out. Think what it will do to your people…'

'Look what it did to ours,' Zakari challenged. 'To our family too—we lost a brother, a son, a royal prince… He must return to the people who love him, who have mourned him needlessly.'

But Xavian wasn't listening. He wanted answers—not just for himself, but for the real Xavian.

'Summon the palace doctor.'

He arrived a short while later, knelt and pleaded for mercy as his sins caught up with him.

'It was the King's order. I was his doctor...'

'You are my doctor too!' Xavian's eyes flashed black with hate. 'I came to you because I thought I was going insane—those dreams...'

'The pills should have stopped them.'

'They were my memories!' Xavian roared. But for now he wasn't thinking of punishment—all he wanted was the truth.

'Tell me everything.'

# CHAPTER TWELVE

PAIN should be private. Some allowances made. Yet soon they would be here.

As Queen Inas Al'Ramiz walked, dazed, along the beach she thought of what now had to happen...

Advisors.

Cameras.

Journalists.

Elders.

More advisors.

And, worse, there would be questions: How long had the young prince been ill? Was this why the public never saw Xavian? Would King Saqr Al'Ramiz now abdicate? Should he make way for his brother, Sheikh Yazan, to rule Qusay, along with his wife, Sheikha Rihana, who had borne three live, healthy sons, with eyes as blue as Xavian's? But there the similarity ended.

How Inas's jealous heart privately loathed their hardiness. Kareef, the eldest—so strong and forceful with his reckless ways. Rafiq—so spoilt, so vigorous and so indulged. And then there was Tahir…such a wild, untamed child.

How Inas had had to paint on her smile at functions and gatherings as Rihana fussed and cooed over her robust brood, while poor Xavian 'rested'.

'Oh, Xavian!'

Inconsolable with grief, Inas stumbled along the beach—she had pleaded with the King, with the palace doctor, for this fraction of time before the world invaded. 'Let me mourn, let me grieve, let me be a mother and not the Queen for just a while longer.'

She had held his little frame till dawn, till he had been prised from her arms—had begged for this brief reprieve on the condition that when she returned the King's chief advisor would be informed, and then his aides, and then the palace staff and then the people.

There was direct access to this private cove from the senior royal suite—stone steps were carved into the shell-studded and jewelled walls of the palace and they led to this rare haven—and Inas had, blind with tears, made her way to the secluded beach, the one place in Qusay where she could just be. No staff were permitted, no cameras could peek— here she could be herself. Here she could wander with a ravaged, tear-streaked face and scream out to a God who hadn't listened.

'Xavian…' She howled his name—felt his soul passing through her, ripping her flesh as it left.

She had loved him so much, would rather lie down and die this minute than carry on living without him.

But she was Queen.

Sedated, she would stand beside her King as he did the honourable thing and abdicated because of her failure to produce an heir. Or, again, they would promise to the people of Qusay, via a spokesperson, that her aching womb would soon produce…

Deranged, Inas wandered, raging at the ocean, at the sky, the sand, the sun, that all carried on when her baby was gone.

She had been told this day would come— the doctor had told her hours after delivery that her desperately awaited son was too weak, too damaged to survive.

Fundamentally a mother, Inas had simply refused to listen, and had spent the next seven years in denial, nurturing her ailing child and shielding him from the gaze of a hungry public. Modern medicine, rare herbs and ancient wisdom had all been frequent visitors to the palace—but to no avail. The seizures had ravaged his body more frequently, Xavian's slender frame had buckled more and more under the sheer effort of staying alive, and of course the rumours had flared—the whispers that the young Prince was sick, weak, and would never be fit to be King had intensified.

They had all been rebuffed.

He would get better. He would be strong.

Inas had been insistent. Had begged Saqr to believe, as she had, that one day Xavian would be well, would rule the Kingdom of Qusay. She had guarded him like a mother lion—yet it hadn't been enough.

Death, the thief that had slipped into the palace tonight, had taken her baby…

She ached to hold him again, ached for him to be still warm…

And now she had to go back. Back to the palace, to face a world without him—except she wouldn't.

Couldn't.

Charging into the ocean, she begged it to claim her—wanted it to take her if it meant she could be with Xavian.

'I miss you, my baby!' she screamed. 'Give me my baby….' she begged, even while knowing it was worthless. After all, she had prayed for years for healthy heirs, for children. In years of trying just one child had been produced, and he had now been ripped from her arms.

There was no God.

She felt the pull of the ocean, felt the waves dragging her out, and then she panicked— realised only then what she was doing. She was Queen, a ruler—there had to be hope, there had to be belief. What lesson was she teaching her people if she let the ocean claim her?

'*Ana asifa…*' she whimpered as she made her way back to shore. 'I am sorry, so sorry. Please show me—show me my path—show me what to do… Show me...'

And there he was…

A shadow on the beach, his dark skin blending with the wet sand, his clothes strewn and torn like seaweed…

She was surely seeing things…

Still waist-deep in the ocean, wading through the crashing waves, Inas knew she must be hallucinating—for there, washed up on the beach, was her child…

It was an illusion, she told herself as she ran towards him. Grief must have driven her insane. Yet the closer she got, the more real he became: thick black curls just like Xavian's after his evening bath, long dark lashes fanning his sallow cheeks. And as she knelt she saw the flutter of his chest, the flicker of black eyelashes, and realised that he was alive.

His wrists were bloodied and wounded, his face sunburnt and bruised, yet despite his state, despite the wounds, he was beautiful— full plum lips, flesh and muscle on his bones. When she pulled his lids open she saw eyes that were inky black, not the signature blue of Al'Ramiz lineage, but Inas disregarded that detail…

This was Xavian, had he been born strong…

God had answered her prayers—had shown her her path—this child had been sent for her!

Scooping him up, she ran to the palace… Time was of the essence, as the deadline to reveal Xavian's death was looming.

She knew deep down this was not Xavian, yet hope was flaring as she stumbled up the stone steps, clutching the body to her bosom until the startled doctor who was still shrouding Xavian pulled the limp child from her arms.

'Xavian...' Inas begged as the doctor worked on him.

'Inas...' The King had tears in his eyes as he pleaded with his wife to see sense. 'This is not Xavian—this is the Sheikh Prince Zafir of Calista. It has been on every news bulletin, in all the papers, I rang King Ashraf myself, to offer the Kingdom of Qusay's prayers....' He realised his wife had been so immersed in their son's declining health that she hadn't heard or taken in the terrible news. 'Three of the Princes were swept out to sea, where they were captured by pirates. Two have escaped, but young Zafir is still missing—they have been searching for him for days...his mother is desperate...'

'*She* is not his mother...' Inas snarled. 'She married the King and took on his sons—how can it be fair that she has five and I have none? She never gave birth. I did...'

'Inas...'

'Who would know?' Inas said—because to

her the solution was simple. 'We will nurse him back to health, he can be our son, and one day he will be Qusay's ruler…'

'Our son is dead.'

'He doesn't have to be.' She ached, yearned, *needed* to be a mother, and God had just shown her how. 'Don't you see? My prayers have just been answered! This was meant to be!'

'Inas, please…' the King begged her. 'This is a Calistan Royal. If we return him to his people it will do our nation good. We will be looked on favourably and it will forge—'

'How can you think of connections at a time like this?' She was demented with fury. She slapped her King as he took her last hope away, and Saqr stood stunned as she hit him again—not with her hand this time, but with words aimed straight at his proud heart. 'Do you really want Yazan to rule? Are you saying you want that tyrant to be King of Qusay?' He had never seen his wife like this. Usually gentle and meek, she was the antithesis now—but, more than that, on this solemn day she was letting hope flare for him, the King, too. He did not want to abdicate, did not want his sadistic brother

Yazan to be King, did not want to relinquish his birthright…

Maybe this *was* the way? Maybe Inas was right and this was meant to be?

'His eyes are not blue…' Saqr said, his voice tentative. 'How would we explain that his eyes are not blue…?' And Inas felt a surge of relief as she realised that, instead of refusing her desperate dream, her King was trying to work out how to fulfil it.

'There have been no portraits,' Inas said quickly. 'The only photo released shows him sleeping…'

'Could we?' The King looked to the doctor, who shook his head.

'Ethically, I cannot allow this…' Dr Habib had put a drip in the limp child and wrapped him in blanket, his face grave with concern. 'We must inform the Calistan palace at once.'

Inas pulled her husband aside, forgetting rules, forgetting how she usually demurred. Her baby was dead so there *were* no rules—here was her chance, her chance to hold a child in her aching arms again, to be a mother. 'So, we must inform our people that your brother Yazan will be King.' Inas stared at her husband and watched him flinch. Oh,

Yazan put on a good façade, but Saqr had told her of the cruel streak in his brother, his true unsavoury nature that belied the man on show. 'Do you want that for your people?'

'Of course not.'

'Then tell the doctor that this *will* happen.' She stood her ground. 'Make it happen—if not for me, then for your people.'

Inas held her breath, shivering and wet and still numb with grief. She watched as her husband, the rightful King, granted her dearest wish.

'You are this royal family's doctor,' the King said. 'And I understand this places you in a difficult position. You will have to visit daily, several times a day, to heal this child, which will necessitate you cutting down on your other work...of course you will be suitably compensated...'

Everyone had scruples, but when the King named a figure Dr Habib, who had three children at a private European school, and a wife who loved to travel well, felt his scruples start to wane.

'I cannot...' the doctor started, and yet he wavered—and not just over the money. He was also too scared to deny his King.

'Can this be done?' the King asked again and, pale and sweating, the doctor nodded.

'I think so.'

'Know so!' the King demanded. 'Tell me how.'

'The people know the Prince is sick. If we keep him hidden for a while longer, it will cause no alarm…'

'Are there rumours of Xavian's death?' the King asked, demanding an honest answer.

'There are rumours that he is gravely ill…' Dr Habib said. 'As this child is.'

'Speak with the advisors…' the King said. 'Tell them that Xavian was taken ill in the night, that more intensive care is required, but that we are hopeful that in time…with proper care…the Prince will make a full recovery.'

'What about Xavian?' asked the doctor. 'What will I do with your son…?' He had expected Inas to start wailing again, but she was nursing the child on the bed, tending to the wounds on his wrists, loving him as she had loved her own son—and Dr Habib saw true denial at work.

'You will deal with him.'

The young Prince was laid to rest and, sick

with guilt, Dr Habib made his way back to the palace to check on his patient—just in time to see Sheikh Prince Zafir open his eyes for the first time.

'Ommah?' The confused child wept for his mother, his eyes struggling to focus, confused and delirious and scared.

'Ommah is here, Xavian,' Inas crooned—and how delicious those words sounded, even as the child wept harder.

And finally, a couple of weeks later, a little bit stronger, his lips redder, his body plumper, one afternoon the young Prince awoke and his eyes fixed on the Queen and the future of Qusay was assured.

'Ommah!'

The brainwashing was complete.

# CHAPTER THIRTEEN

'WHERE is he?' Xavian demanded. He could feel cold nausea drenching him. 'Where is the real Xavian…?'

'Your Highness…' Akmal was wringing his hands. 'Better to let him rest…'

'Where does he rest?' Xavian demanded. 'In the royal cemetery?' He was almost dizzy. 'I want to go there…' He snapped his fingers. 'Akmal, arrange transport…'

The royal cemetery was close to the palace, at the next headland, a short drive away. Gated and guarded, it was open to the public only occasionally—the last time had been the day after his parents' burial, and Xavian was not looking forward to returning, but it was imperative he go now…

'He is not there.' The doctor was so pale it looked as if *he* needed a doctor.

'Then where…?' Xavian demanded of Akmal. 'You will tell me where he is.'

'Sire, I know nothing of this…'

'Akmal speaks the truth…' The doctor interrupted Akmal's plea. 'No one does. It was between your parents and me.'

'My parents?' Xavian's voice was like the crack of a whip. 'They were not my parents. Where is Xavian?'

'They asked that I take care of things…' The doctor was on his knees, begging for forgiveness that could never come. 'When orphans die, there is a place on the edge of the desert…'

'The paupers' cemetery?' Xavian bellowed.

Akmal again broke with protocol and urged the King to be quiet, but Xavian was having none of it. 'You are telling me that the Royal Prince Xavian was buried in an unmarked pauper's grave? Take me now.'

He was reeling, angry, confused—he shrugged off Zakari and Stefania, he spat at the doctor, and it was Akmal who drove. He felt as if he was the one who had been buried, and when they reached the graveyard he stood and stared at himself, at a life, a person that had been so easily discarded—a child who had been buried and forgotten.

'Your Highness…' Akmal pleaded with him to return to the car, for this awful night to be over, for the truth to return to the bottle so he could push the cork back in. 'King Xavian…' he begged. 'We must—' Only he never got to finish.

'This is Xavian.' His black eyes held Akmal's and he saw the fear in him, as only then did the true horror of the lie unfold. 'And he will be named and honoured—he will have a royal grave…'

'No...' begged Akmal. 'If this gets out, if the truth is revealed… Do you not see what it will do to our people? Not only will there be no King, but they will lose the loving memories they have of your parents. Sire, this will kill the spirit of Qusay. We must live the lie. Please, I beg you to reconsider—think this through when you are calm.'

As they drove through the black night, Xavian realised he did have to think it through.

It was all he could agree to.

He walked along the beach where he had been washed up, and now he understood.

That speck he had sought on the horizon had been himself.

The ocean he had loathed so much had brought him to Qusay.

He had always known.

Somewhere, locked inside, it had always been there, tapping away, trying to get out. He walked along the beach where he had been delivered that fateful morning to his mother, to Inas… He stared out at that vast ocean and wondered how he, a child alone, had survived—and for a terrifying moment he wondered if it would have been easier to have died. In many ways he had. He had his identity, everything, ripped from him. Even his age was different. Zakari had told him his birth date—he was twenty-eight, not twenty-nine.

And the real Xavian, the child he mourned now, was not even his brother.

Everything that he was, everything he knew, had gone.

Xavian, King Xavian, son of Inas and Saqr—all of that was gone.

So who was he?

Years were wiped out—his childhood gone. Every word of praise, every time he had been told he was loved, it had not been said to him, but to a ghost.

The people of Qusay would be shattered—and there was his wife…

Was Layla *even* his wife? She had married someone who did not exist.

Always Xavian had felt it was duty that made him different, always he had stood apart—arrogant, some said; aloof, said others. There had been no friends, no socialising even with other royals, apart from brief visits with cousins—and now he knew why.

Slowly over the years he had been brainwashed.

He could see Layla walking along the private beach towards him, still dressed in her nightgown, barefoot, her face swollen from crying. The rising sun was behind her, and he could see her silhouette thought the flimsy fabric. He would have killed for escape, to lie her down on the sand and shower that tear-stained face with kisses.

They had made love—more than that, they had found love. For the first time Xavian had let a woman in to a place in his heart, only to shut her out now—for if he did as Akmal pleaded, if he did choose to live this lie, then he must do it alone. He could not burden her with the weight he might carry.

The truth would shatter her and her people, *his* people, and ruin so many lives—his life too, for he wanted to be King. He had been groomed to be King, and now that he was he relished it—the decisions, the power, his Kingdom, his people. He was a good King, a very good King, and he didn't want to walk away from it.

Could he live a lie?

'Come to bed, Xavian...' She had never once pleaded, never begged, but she was scared now—scared of what she didn't know. She had spent a sleepless night, walked the palace corridors listening to cars driving away and raised voices. Baja had shooed her back to bed, but still she had not slept. Walking out to the balcony to get some air, she had seen Xavian pacing the beach, his royal robes wet and sandy, billowing behind him, his *kafeya* gone. Even from a distance she could sense his anger, his pain, and she wanted to share it. 'What is wrong?'

'I don't want to talk.'

'Then don't talk,' Layla compromised. 'But come inside—come to bed...'

'I want to be alone.'

'No.' She refused to hear it. 'We said we would talk after the reception—that we would discuss things, that we would share…'

'That day can wait,' Xavian said. 'Akmal is packing.' She was holding his wrists, trying to make eye contact, but he didn't look at her. 'I have been invited to stay as a guest at Calista.'

'That is good…' she reasoned. 'We can have some time—'

'Just me.' Xavian interrupted. 'Only I have been invited.'

'No…'

'Layla…it has been good.' He peeled her warm body from his. 'But as we both know this is business arrangement: you rule Haydar.' She was shaking her head, refusing to believe that so soon he could take all his promises back. 'Right now there is an opportunity for Qusay to improve relations with Calista and Aristo—the Kingdom of Adamas has long been out of bounds to us, and it will be good for our people in the long run…'

'But not good for us.' They had been married just a week, the most wonderful week of her life, and he had told her things would be different, had made love to her over and over. She had been so deeply intimate with him, and yesterday he had shown her how different, how much better their lives could be, and now he was ripping it all away.

'Yesterday you promised that soon we would share things…' she insisted. 'Xavian, let me be there for you.'

He would not do that to her. It was better that she hated him—because soon, very soon, he might have to tell her and his country the truth, or live with a permanent lie between them.

There was nothing that could be salvaged—they simply couldn't win.

'Please don't go without me, Xavian.'

'Do you know what I liked about you, Layla? Do you know what made you different?'

She just stood there.

'Begging does not suit you. I preferred it when you kept me guessing.'

He could see her shape beneath her nightdress. Her face was beautiful without makeup, her breasts full and ripe, and despite his bold statement of earlier this was not mere business. He was hard now. He wanted to drag her down on the sand beside him and make love to her right there. He tried to battle with his mind, which was urging him to kiss her. He stared at her mouth, and instinct—impulse, anger—had his hands in her hair. Had him pulling her face towards him, wishing, wishing he had never found out the truth, had lived in the bliss of ignorance, where he could properly taste her.

She jerked her head back. That he could shame her and then kiss her enraged her so—that he thought she was a puppet to play with, to dance to his will—well, she was better than that, stronger than that... So she stepped out of the dance, so she could claim back herself, and he knew then that it was over.

'I need to go to Calista,' Xavian said. 'Alone.'

And Layla thought she understood.

'Is this something that will benefit the people of Qusay only? Something you would not like to share with Haydar?'

He did not answer her, and Layla decided Baja was right: it was all about duty for him—and so it must be for her.

'Just as there was a formal function here in Qusay, my people will expect the same. I did not shame you, and yet now you ask me to return without my groom…to become a bride who does not bring her husband home even for a few nights…'

'People know it is business…'

'They do not need it rubbed in their faces.'

'We will say we are in the desert…' Finally a small compromise. 'You will remain here.'

'Here?'

'Or you can spend time in the desert until I return…'

'No!' She would not return there without him—could not stand to sleep alone in the bed where they had made love—and no more would she beg him.

'Go and do your deal in Calista—but I am not going to stay locked in a palace pretending for ever. You have a week. If you choose, after that, not to return to Haydar for a respectable time, if you choose to dishonour me in that way, then never ask me to stand as your wife in anything other than duty.'

She pushed him from her then—pushed him as if he revolted her.

'Sort it out, Xavian—you have one week.'

## CHAPTER FOURTEEN

Now that he had let himself remember, memories returned with a vengeance. And as he stepped into the Calistan palace, it was as if he was being pelted with them.

He could hear his mother's laughter, and his own boyish giggles as he chased that bird that had flown into the palace. He could see himself running along the corridors, opening doors that he had always but never known... And later, out in the stables, he buried his face in the neck of a fierce stallion named Death, inhaled the scent of the stables and felt giddy with recall.

'My parents forbade me to ride...' Xavian said. 'As the only heir I had to be responsible. One day I defied them and rode the fiercest horse in the stable—I saddled him myself, and I mounted him easily. I could not understand how I knew what to do...I just did.'

'You were like a gypsy boy.' Zakari smiled. 'You loved your horses.' He paused for a moment. 'All this is yours, Zafir.'

'Don't call me that.'

'You *are* Zafir.'

'It will kill my people.'

'I do not care for your people,' Zakari said. 'Qusay stole my brother—it has had enough borrowed time; I feel no guilt that we claim what is ours.'

'What about my wife?' Xavian roared. 'She married a king.'

'And now she gets a prince...' Zakari shrugged. 'You can help her...'

'Help her!' Xavian gave a black laugh. 'She does not need my help—she rules her way...'

'Then let her,' Zakari said, as if it were that simple. 'Everyone knows this is nothing more than a business arrangement—she can get on with ruling Haydar; you can get on with being Prince. Anyway...' Zakari shrugged '...the marriage may not even be legal now...'

It was like a knife to his chest.

'You can have your life back, Zafir—the life Qusay has denied you, the life that was meant for you. Come now...' Zakari said. 'It is time to inform your brothers...'

'No!' Xavian halted him. 'Not yet. I will decide in my own time.'

'They have missed you; they have grieved…'

'A few days' more will make no difference.'

And at least Zakari granted him that.

# CHAPTER FIFTEEN

DESPITE her brave words to him, Layla could not cleanse herself of want.

She tried so hard—tried to simply hate him.

Each morning as Baja bathed her the henna butterfly he had kissed faded a little. She filled her days with reading, with long walks on the beach, she wrote morose pages in her diary as she awaited his return—but at night she burned for him. She wished she had never known him, because up till then she had slept. Now her body twitched like a jumble of electric wires, nerves all awakened, all missing what just a week ago they had never even known.

She had given him a week—and still, as always, he made her wait.

And she gave him another day, because...well, because she had to.

But when by day nine there was still no word, no sign of his return, she could take it no more.

She had a right to better than this, and so she summoned Akmal.

'Arrange my flight. Let my people know I am returning to Haydar.'

'Perhaps a couple more days, Your Highness…'

How dared he suggest that to her? How dared an aide of the absent King, suggest what she might do?

'You will arrange for my things to be packed.' Layla was pale with rage at his insolence. 'And summon my plane.'

'There are papers that need your signature— both your signatures—with witnesses…'

'Tell that to your King.'

'It will not look good…' She was about to demand that he leave, and to have him reprimanded severely, yet his eyes were filled with tears. In abject apology he knelt on the floor and pleaded—pleaded with Her Majesty to give his master some more time. 'He has so much to contend with….'

'Like what?' she demanded, because till Stefania and Zakari had asked for an audience things had been perfect—well, not perfect, but better than this. 'He is busy brokering a deal that will serve you, Akmal, and your people,'

'This is not about stones or jewels.' The vizier bowed his head.

For Akmal to reveal even this much had her heart tripping with fear. 'Then what?' she croaked, and then cleared her voice. 'What is it that my husband is struggling so hard to contend with?' But even as she asked she knew that the loyal Akmal's first duty was to his King. Yet his answer was more telling than she had expected.

'Your husband appears to treat you poorly…' Akmal's lips trembled at his own indiscretion. 'For a King to leave his Queen alone so soon…' His eyes pleaded with her to listen, to read between the lines, to do *something*, because this was more weight than Akmal could bear. 'Yet I believe he will return soon, that all will be well, if you can just give him some time…'

She was scared for her husband.

Layla stood there and was scared.

Was he being bribed? The moods, the nightmares…? Her scalp was tight with fear.

But Xavian was strong.

What was it that troubled him so?

She had to know.

'There is a change of plan—I am going to Calista…' She watched Akmal's eyes widen. 'Unannounced,' she warned, and so determined was she that Akmal nodded. 'I will remind your King of the consequences should he choose not to return to my country with me…'

For the first time in days Akmal had hope. He had never seen Xavian so smitten with a woman—maybe Queen Layla *could* be the one to persuade him. For if he lost Qusay he would lose her too—the Queen of Haydar would surely prefer to be married to a King!

'You cannot go to him yet…' As she opened her mouth to reprimand him, Akmal bravely spoke over her. 'Your eyes are swollen from crying, your hair is unkempt, and I know how King Xavian likes…' His voice trailed off, but she did not reprimand him. They were both on the same side after all—they both wanted him back, both wanted the world to be as it had been just a few days ago. 'Let me help you, Your Highness.'

And she nodded.

Maybe it could work, Akmal thought as he ran around, clapping hands, summoning staff. He called the beautician, make-up artists, the finest designers—oh, when King Xavian saw his bride surely that would bring him home…

'Not yet!' Baja called, as Akmal knocked at the door—but the Queen overrode her, allowing Xavian's vizier the final say.

'Will I do?'

Though he had never found love himself, Akmal decided that there was surely nothing more beautiful than a woman who was in love.

She had chosen well. Her pale skin was enhanced by a dress so black it was almost blue, made in a silk so heavy it looked like wool, and it clung to her curves. The empress neckline enhanced her bust, her legs looked even longer in high-heeled black shoes, and her hair, usually worn down, was instead piled high on her head, with some stray curls tumbling down. It was divine—surely the King's impulse would be the same as any man's? To pull out the grips and watch her hair fall like a theatre curtain. Her cheeks were accentuated with blusher, her lips skilfully rouged, and her eyes darkened with kohl.

She looked both shy and wanton, and Akmal decided if anything would silence the King, if anything would make him stay, then it stood now before him.

'You will bring our King home,' Akmal said, which was a soaring compliment to Layla. 'Wear this…' He handed her the emerald necklace Xavian had given her on the night of the official ceremony. 'This means everything to our people, to the royal family… When he sees you in this…'

It dripped between her breasts, and even Baja found she was smiling—from tomboy princess, to hard nosed Queen, to shy bride. Today her Layla was all woman—a woman dressed for her husband's eyes. But now she must dress for others, and Baja helped her put on her veil.

'We are ready,' Baja said to Akmal, but Layla had other plans.

'No, Baja. I am going to Calista alone.'

'You do not know what you will find there…' Baja said, because King Xavian's reputation was legendary. 'You should have someone with you.'

'I will face him alone,' Layla said, because Baja confused her. 'And if he chooses not to return…'

Akmal closed his eyes for a moment—he knew the truth; he knew what she was walking into.

'I will escort you,' Akmal said.

'He could fire you…' Layla pointed out. 'He may be furious at my arrival. You do not have to risk your job…'

'I am coming with you.'

The journey took four hours. She wanted her arrival to be unannounced, so instead of landing at the palace the royal plane touched down at Calista Airport, where a luxury car took her through ancient streets to a place she had never been.

She was grateful that Akmal was with her, because there was some difficulty at the palace gates. It was Akmal who smoothed the way, assuring them that, yes, indeed it was Queen Layla who had just arrived to join her husband, and he suggested it would be extremely rude to keep her waiting.

After just a moment or two the gates opened and Layla was invited in.

'You can go back to the plane,' Layla offered, 'Xavian does not need to know that you brought me here.'

'I will wait for you,' Akmal said stoutly. 'You go inside. I know several of King Zakari's aides; I will pass the time talking with them.'

A rather flustered Queen Stefania greeted her in the lounge as a nanny swept a tearful baby away.

'Forgive me.' Queen Stefania stood. 'I was feeding baby Zafir; we were not expecting you…Zafir did not…' She stopped talking and shook her head. 'Sorry, Xavian did not…'

'You can carry on feeding Zafir,' Layla said. 'I am sorry to interrupt that.'

'He had just finished,' Stefania said. 'Xavian did not say to expect you…'

'Xavian does not know.'

'Can I get you some tea…?' She nodded to a maid. 'Some refreshments…?'

'I just want to speak with my husband.'

'Please…' Stefania gestured. 'Won't you have a seat?'

'No, thank you.' There must have been something in her voice that told Stefania that polite royal talk was not going to appease

Layla. She would not sit, she had not even taken off her veils, she just stood there, strong and defiant and almost…dangerous. There was a recklessness in Layla that Stefania recognised from a time in her own life—no matter who was present, she would speak her mind. Clearly worried, Stefania dismissed her maid as a precaution.

'He is out riding…' Stefania said. 'I am sure if you had let us know you were coming he would have been here…'

'When will he return?' Layla watched as the Queen ran a worried hand through her hair. She was clearly embarrassed, and Layla did not want to hurt her, but she was hurting herself.

'I am sorry, I don't know. Perhaps we could go for a walk in the gardens…?'

'A walk!' Layla was sick of this—sick of the games, sick of the double talk. As if she could walk in the manicured gardens and make stupid conversation about flowers and such! 'I did not come here to walk. I am here to see my husband. To find out why, one week after our wedding, he chooses to spend time getting to know your family rather than his bride.'

'There are perhaps things that the Kings need to discuss…'

'Is this a joke? Layla demanded. 'Or is this acceptable to you? I suppose it must be…' Layla scoffed as Stefania closed her eyes. Layla dished out the truth. 'After all, you invited only *him* to join you here in Calista. Am I wrong to want to see my husband?'

'Of course not…' Stefania was weeping, remembering the hell of her own honeymoon, when Zakari had told her theirs was a marriage of convenience only—when she had found out he had married her only so that he could claim the Karedes Diamond. She could hear the pain in Layla's voice, the confusion and anger, and Stefania recognised it as if it were her own. Oh, she had supported her husband on this—theirs was a strong and loving marriage now, and on everything except this Zakari listened to her. But not where his long-lost brother was concerned. For Zakari it was simple: Zafir must return home. But here before Stefania was just a fraction of the pain that decision might bring. And she admired Layla too—how brave she was to stand in an unfamiliar palace and demand her rights as a wife.

'I want to see my husband,' Layla said

finally. 'I'm sorry if it makes you uncomfortable, or if it is an imposition, but I am not leaving until I do.' Only then did she sit down, and Stefania knew that Layla was not going anywhere until she got answers.

'He went out on Death before dawn.'

'Death…'

'The stallion. We told him it was not advisable, but he is not keen to listen to anyone now… He has been gone since…'

'I don't believe you. I want you to take me to my husband.'

'He is riding…' But it was dark now; the sun had set hours ago.

Layla shook her head at the impossibility. 'Xavian doesn't ride; his parents forbade it— that much I do know about him. So he cannot possibly be out on a stallion.'

'Please, Layla,' Stefania begged. 'Zakari has gone out looking for him. I am on your side. I want you to talk to Xavian…'

'Then you will show me to the stables…

'You cannot go out…'

'I am not going out looking for him….' Layla corrected her assumption. 'I will wait for his return—before you and your husband get to him, or speak on my behalf….'

* * *

Layla was worried, and terribly so.

Out after dark, on a beast of a horse—he could be lying with his neck broken... She refused Stefania's offer to join her and instead followed her directions to the luxurious riding complex, past an indoor, air-conditioned arena where a young prince was practising his jumps, and then through to the stables area. Clearly horses played a large part in the Al'Farisi royal family's lives, because it was modern, airy and gleaming—but none of that would keep Xavian safe out riding in the dark. What on earth had he been thinking?

She waited for ages.

The young prince had long since finished, his horse safely stabled for the night, and the lights to the arena were turned off. Layla paced Death's stable, worried for Xavian, and worried for herself too, when he found out she had come to confront him.

And then she heard him—or at least she heard one set of hooves that could be Zakari's horse. But no, as she looked over the stable door it *was* Xavian...

Neither exhausted nor weary, he dismounted from the beast and led it to the yard, hosing down his legs and tying him up before he removed the saddle, leaving the rest for one of the stablehands to do. In the darkness Layla removed her veils and stood watching her King's approach, wondering what his reaction would be when he found out she was here.

He had ridden all day, had galloped at breakneck speed through the desert, and yet had found nothing—no peace, no clarity, just anger: a burning fury. He was sick of Zakari, of Stefania, of them telling him what he must do, guiding him—they could all go to hell.

No one knew. No one knew how torn he was.

'Xavian…'

He opened the door, flicked on the light and there she was, standing in a black dress and black stilettos, her legs bare, her hair in wild black ringlets, with the necklace of the rightful Qusay Queen around her neck—except the rules didn't apply any more.

'My plane is waiting at the airport.'

'So?' He strode past her and threw down the saddle.

'If you do not return with me to Qusay then I leave for Haydar tonight.'

'Then go.'

'There are papers we need to sign. There are things we need to discuss.'

'I have nothing to discuss and I do not do paperwork in a stable…' He turned to where she stood, ran his eyes across her naked arms and legs, the generous glimpse of cleavage, and all he wanted was her. All he wanted to do was live the lie—to take her to bed with him this night and go back to what they'd had.

But living a lie was not honourable…

'Xavian?'

Something inside him twisted—because she didn't even know his name.

'When you are more suitably dressed you can join me in the palace and we will do business.'

'I don't want to go to the palace.'

'What *do* you want?' His question was urgent. 'What is it you want from me? Tell me now.'

'What we had,' Layla said.

Only Xavian knew that could never be.

'You want a king?'

'No!' Layla shook her head, her curls catching the light, confused by his questions. 'I want you, Xavian. It is you I want.'

'Me?' What a joke—she didn't even know who he was. He kicked the stable door closed behind him. 'You know nothing of me!' Xavian roared. 'Yet you demand everything. This was business…it was agreed; now you have decided to change the rules.'

'We decided!' Layla's shout matched his. 'When we made love, when we kissed, when we spoke—that was not business…'

'So you are complaining that I was too nice to you? That the sex was too good…?'

'You are twisting my words…' She refused to just turn tail and run, and how Xavian admired her for that—but how he feared for her too. Because of the shame that this scandal would cause and also, in a deeper truth, because he did not want to see the disappointment in her eyes when she found out who he was.

'I don't want business. I don't want separate lives—you with mistresses, with other women. I want you all for me…' Layla tried to voice her confusion, but Xavian could stand it no more.

'So you come here dressed as a slut?'

'How would you prefer me to dress?' Layla demanded. 'You *made* me this,

Xavian. I was prepared just for sex, but you demanded more…you brought out the woman in me—and now you are sending her back; now you want a meek, compliant virgin. Well, she is gone!'

'Go!' he shouted. 'Go back to the palace.'

'I don't want to go back!' She was begging again—she was Queen and she never begged, but she could stand this no more. 'I want you to make love to me…'

'Well, why didn't you just say?' Xavian shouted, walking towards her unzipping his jodhpurs. She saw his fierce erection, and then she felt his mouth, savage and hard on hers… He was pushing her to the ground, his hands everywhere, his body a solid weight on her, pinning her down, sliding the heavy silk dress up, tearing at her panties, crushing her with his mouth, his knees pushing at her thighs—and then he stopped.

'Is this what you want?' he demanded, and he was as close to crying as he had ever come. Better that he shouted.

'You know it's not.'

His face buried in her neck felt the cool of the necklace, the centuries of tradition. All this he could keep, along with the woman in his arms, if he could remain silent, if he did not tell her his truth.

'What is it you want?'

'You.'

'I cannot be King…'

This time when she heard this strong man's desperation she did not act as a queen, because she had learnt that lesson already. She did not demand answers. Instead she acted as his lover, because she knew that this was terrible—knew she could not think, because if she thought then she must speak.

It was Layla kissing him now, frantic kisses to chase away what must come later. She knew he was hurting, was scared for him too—and so she wrenched him for the last time from the black place he visited, and it was just two of them again. She actually believed they could work it out, and her body, far from fighting him, was accepting him, matching the frenzy of his want…

'I want you,' Layla said, and for now she had him. He was inside her. And yet she wanted more—she didn't want to climax because she knew then it would be over, but her body was alive and she tried to subdue it. He was pushing hard into her, and her body beat for him, dragged him in, and still she fought it. But she was gripping him tight with her centre, her hands pushing him deeper in as her contrary mind fought for just a few more moments. But he was shuddering his release, and her body sobbed and matched his. The ferocity of her orgasm didn't alarm her, but she lay there stunned and reeling as his weight collapsed on her. Its intensity seemed suitable, somehow, because at some level Layla knew it would be their last.

This passion, this need, this want couldn't be sustained by one person, and she knew in her heart that Xavian was about to sign himself out of the deal that was *them*.

He was surprisingly tender afterwards. He kissed her. He helped her stand. He helped her dress and brushed the sawdust from her dress and from his clothes too. The angry, loaded man who had walked into the stables had gone—if anything he looked exhausted, world-weary, yet somehow proud, and for the first time since she had seen him he looked her in the eyes.

'There are some formalities that need to be completed. I must return to Qusay for a short while, and of course you must return to

Haydar, and…' He paused, expected a question, for Layla to interrupt—except she didn't, and he could not have been more proud of her. He could see that she was steeling herself for whatever he was going to say to her. 'If you still want to remain married we will resume our original deal—except I will be living in Calista…'

'Calista?' Now she did question him. She had prepared herself for the fact he did not want her, that he did not want to rule her land, and she would accept that with grace, but this she did not understand—his words made absolutely no sense. 'What do you mean, if I want to remain married? There can be no divorce…'

'I am not King Xavian of Qusay. I am the missing Sheikh Prince Zafir of Calista.'

'I don't understand…' Layla whispered. 'Xavian…'

'My name is Zafir…' he corrected. 'Which means our marriage is not binding. The Xavian you married does not exist. I never was him. I am not your husband.'

# CHAPTER SIXTEEN

'WE SEARCHED for years…'

They were in the Calistan palace. Layla
sat shivering, sipping camomile tea to calm
her shredded nerves, but it did nothing—her
knees still bobbed up and down. Stefania had
wrapped a cloak around her shoulders, and
the room was warm, but she could not stop
shivering. She knew deep inside just how
devastating this was for so many people, yet
her mind was not quite ready to fathom the
enormity of it in one swoop. Gently Zakari
and Stefania helped her join up the dots,
but Xavian—or rather Zafir—sat in stony
silence. He was still in his jodhpurs, his
clothes filthy from a day's riding, sawdust in
his hair, and all Layla wanted to do was cross
the room and sit with him, to hold his hand
as Zakari gave her the painful details. But

there was an invisible shield around him, a detachment, a barrier that guarded him, and Layla knew all she could do was listen, and try to push aside the devastating personal loss. Her mind, even in such desperate times, had to think first of her kingdom.

Zakari went on. 'My father spared no expense. Though logic said he must be dead, still there was hope he was alive somewhere—there were detectives, the underworld was infiltrated, and there were even rumours he had been adopted. Every kingdom was searched…' Zakari's lips were taut in bitter rage. 'My father even spoke with the King of Qusay—he offered his full assistance…'

He turned to his brother, who just stared fixedly ahead. 'Every day you were missed. It is time to come home now.'

'How?' Zafir's voice was not helpless; instead it demanded answers. 'My people will be crushed. They are already in mourning. And what about the people of Haydar…?' He looked over to Layla. 'You kissed a king and he turned into a prince...'

'The people of Haydar will welcome—'

'Please…' Zafir sneered. 'I am no Queen's

consort. I do not need some honorary role.' He stood and crossed the room to stare out of the windows. Unlike the place he had called home, it did not look out onto the ocean, but the desert, and yet it did not soothe him. Maybe one day it would—in time perhaps this might feel like home. After all, the palace at Qusay never had.

'Could you excuse us?' he asked of his brother and sister-in-law. But when they were alone it took a while for either of them to speak.

Layla stood now, no longer shivering. She was too busy thinking. She was used to making tough decisions in moments, used to weighing up options, exploring possibilities and coming to rapid conclusions—but this was the hardest thing her mind had explored. When he went to interrupt her thoughts, when he opened his mouth to speak, Layla closed her eyes, so he stayed silent until she opened them again, with her decision made.

'I will lie for you.'

He winced as she said it, saw the tears stream down her cheeks as she risked honour and reputation and the people she loved to climb into this lie with him. He wouldn't let her do it.

'No.'

'I will lie—you can trust that I will never reveal your secret.'

'No!'

'Akmal will never say anything. You can surely persuade your brother…'

'No!' he shouted.

Alone, he might have lied, but he would not do it with her.

'Layla…' He did not look at her now, just stared out into the dark night. 'I will have my people look into it, but if the marriage is binding—which I doubt—then I will offer you an annulment.'

'I don't want an annulment…'

'I married you out of duty.' Zafir's words were cruel, but that was the only way he could do this—the only way he could fall from grace with just a shred of dignity. 'That duty no longer exists.'

'What about my honour?'

'I am prepared to say that the marriage was never consummated. That we found out the truth about my identity on our wedding day and have spent time working out what to do…'

'Oh!' Layla stood and scoffed. 'And I thought we were trying to halt the lies…silly me. Like it or not, the marriage was consummated—we are married.'

'As you wish.' Zafir shrugged.

'So will you come with me to Haydar?'

'And take your orders?'

'I would have to teach you our ways.'

'Teach me…' His lips curled in distaste. 'Would you double-check my work? Would you have to sign off on that too…?'

'I don't know…' Layla admitted, because she was Queen, and had ruled for a long time, and had never envisaged sharing to this extent.

'And read over my speeches…?' Zafir persisted.

'No.' She was crying now.

'And then I reward you for letting me play at being King by sleeping with you at night?'

He couldn't—he could not take her crumbs.

He had had power, and, guess what? He had loved it—just as she did.

'I would rather be a prince.'

'Than be with me?'

'Layla, from as far back as I can remember I have without question accepted my duty—ruling was my future, my passion. Now that that is not an option—well, a prince's life sounds good. I do not have the weight of a country on my shoulders, and I have a whole family waiting. I can ride horses, play polo...'

'Screw tarts...'

'High-class tarts,' Zafir corrected, but though he said it he could not fathom it. Somehow those days were over for him. No matter how brave his words, the thought of a woman who was not Layla—well, he couldn't bring himself to even consider it. 'I will be discreet, and of course I will service you—I will give you your promised heir...' He frowned as he did the maths—they had been married more than two weeks now, and their wedding night had been at her most fertile time. 'Perhaps I already have.'

She said nothing, just stood there as he called in Stefania and Zakari, and Akmal too. His decision had been made; now all he had to was carry it through.

'My decision is made. Tonight I am returning to Qusay. I want to arrange a dignified resting place for Xavian—but the people do not need to know how thoughtlessly he was discarded. Once that has taken place, I will inform the people as to what has occurred.'

'How will you tell them?' Layla's face was pale.

'On national television,' Zafir answered. 'In the next couple of days, as soon as Xavian is in his rightful resting place, and before rumours start to spread. I will contact Kareef and tell him that he is the rightful King…'

'I will tell my people after you.' Layla's eyes were wide in her bleached face. She thought of Kareef, and of the news he would soon receive, of how so many lives would be changed. 'And then I will return to Haydar…'

'Alone,' Zafir reminded her. 'I need time with my family, but of course I will visit in due course…' He could not stand the thought of her people, of their prying eyes as the deposed King stepped off the plane. His shame was intense, he felt emasculated, but he would never, ever let her see that.

'I miss being a prince.'

She gave a tight smile. 'Then a prince you shall be—as I said, I will inform my people.'

'Please do,' Zafir said coolly, finding it safer to keep her at a distance. 'I will leave for Qusay now. There is a lot to do.'

'You are welcome to stay here, Layla,'

Stefania offered, when he did not suggest that she join him. 'Till the broadcast…'

She couldn't stand the thought of sleeping in separate chambers, of sharing his palace and not his bed, so gratefully she nodded.

# CHAPTER SEVENTEEN

ZAKARI and Stefania were wonderful hosts.

They accepted she was in shock, and food was brought to her room. Stefania, kind and gentle, sat on her bed in the early hours of her final morning there, and baby Zafir lay between them, kicking his little fat legs, smiling and cooing, utterly oblivious to the pain all around.

They were all to fly to Qusay. Zakari and Stefania would attend the funeral, while Layla waited back at the Qusay palace, and then the truth would be revealed.

'There will be celebrations in the streets here in Calista later...' Layla was still wearing her nightgown, her hair knotted, her eyes swollen from tears. 'And there will be wailing in Qusay.'

'What about Haydar?'

'I don't know,' Layla confessed, and then she admitted just a little more. 'They are not happy under my rule.'

'It would be the same here in Calista,' Stefania admitted. 'They would struggle to accept just a queen. Aristo is more modern, but even there I know that Zakari makes it easier for them to accept me.'

It was such a relief to talk, and Layla wished their friendship had developed under different circumstances. 'With Zafir by my side it would have been so much easier...' Layla whispered, and it felt strange to use his name—it all felt strange. Tears filled her eyes as Stefania sadly shook her head.

'I heard him talking with Zakari. He is King or nothing—his pride will not let him be otherwise…'

When little Zafir started crying it was Layla who picked him up. She felt his cries give way and wished his namesake was as uncomplicated…wished she could comfort him too. But her sympathy would only make things worse.

'I knew the trouble this would cause,' Stefania said sadly. 'I knew how confusing this would be for Zafir. I was raised as a poor girl—I was a palace maid when I found out

I was actually Queen…' She screwed her eyes closed as she recalled her own confusion. 'But it is so much worse for Zafir. At least I knew my mother, and I still had my identity, I still had some truths. Zafir has none.' She looked over to Layla. 'I wasn't going to tell Zakari my suspicions. I was worried that if I was wrong I would have raised his hopes for nothing, and I was scared for Zafir too… But then...' she touched her baby's cheek '…after he was born, when I saw my husband hold him, saw that proud man cry over his name, I knew I had to tell him my thoughts. Zakari has been trying to contact him since. We invited him to stay with us when his parents died—Zakari wanted to see for himself, and we hoped that his being back in Calista would bring memories back—but Xavian, or rather Zafir, failed to respond to our letters, which was unusual, of course. Our kingdom is powerful—Zafir not returning our letters told us he must know something…'

'I think he was starting to.' Layla looked back on their rows with hindsight.

'I wonder if Inas and Saqr had any idea of the pain this would cause…'

'I doubt it...' Stefania said wisely. 'They were probably trying to spare pain at the time.'

But all they had done was pass it on, and it had multiplied and multiplied again. It would do so a thousandfold today, but then hopefully it would end.

The funeral for Xavian was small, but loaded with love.

Zafir had never warmed to Akmal, always he had found him old-fashioned, set in his ways, but seeing the proud man weep, seeing how this day affected him, Zafir got a taste of what was to come for the people of Qusay.

Stefania and Zakari stood with him, yet their togetherness only exacerbated his isolation.

Xavian was placed with his parents—Zafir had said no at first, but had taken counsel from his elder brother and understood he might regret that decision later—so finally Xavian rested where he belonged.

Zafir saw his name, his past, his future—all buried now.

And then he saw Layla approach the small gathering.

She was dressed in a smart black suit, a

simple black lace veil covering her face, but he would have recognised her anywhere— and she was wearing the emeralds.

'You were not invited.'

'I have my respects to pay too…' She stood beside him. 'For as long as I remember Xavian was my betrothed.'

At every turn there was pain. This fracture in the soul of Qusay would spread like an earthquake soon, ripping the foundations of this proud land. She took off the necklace that had been given with love, she was sure, and returned it.

'I will pass it on to Kareef.'

'I hope it brings his wife more happiness than it did me.' Then she saw that his fingers were over the ring she had given him.

'I told you before you accepted my stone—this goes with you to the grave. At least that is the Haydar way. What you do with that tradition is your choice.'

'Layla.' Zafir refused to be manipulated. 'You speak as if you went into the mines and chose it yourself—you speak as if you chose that stone for me. You did not even know me then…'

'Correct,' Layla said. 'I had to respect my

parents' choice for me—even if it meant giving my gift to a man I felt nothing for, even if he repulsed me…' She stared at him, and now they were not talking about the stone. 'Still that gift would have been given. What my husband chooses to do with it now…' She swallowed down sudden tears. 'I am proud to come from Haydar—when we give a gift, it is for ever…' She glanced at the emeralds in his hand to prove her point. 'Know one thing…' He waited for a slap, a spit, for deserved cruel words, but they never came. 'We could work this out together. I love you, Zafir.'

But Zafir didn't know himself—so how could she love him? He was tired of platitudes, of Zakari and Stefania stifling him with those words, of his brothers waiting, of love that was unconditional just because of his name, of love that bound Layla through marriage.

'Love,' Zakari said as he held the cool stones in his palm, 'was not part of the arrangement.'

'No,' Layla agreed—and that was that. She would beg no more, and just hope that in time she would miss him less. 'Let's get this day over with, and then I will return to Haydar…'

\* \* \*

The cars sped them the short distance back to the palace, where they were greeted by a worried Akmal. 'I have spoken with the elders. They think the news must not come from you—that if I speak first…'

'I will tell the people myself!' Zafir was insistent—this was the last thing he could do for his people, and it was something he was brave enough to take on.

'Please…' Akmal pleaded. 'They will not hear you; they will not be comforted—the shock, the fear will set in, and they will not take in your wise words. Please, Sire—let me tell them, let me speak to the press. And then, when they are demanding answers, needing more, you can tell them what will now happen…' Akmal took out a handkerchief and blew his nose. 'What *will* happen?' he begged.

It was only now that the shock was wearing off, and acceptance was seeping in that Zafir realised Akmal was right: he was trying to think of the future. It was right that when the people needed leadership and guidance it should be Zafir who stepped in—that they heard from their King even if for the last time.

'Make the announcement.' Zafir gave the

order. 'Tell the press I will speak with the nation before sunset.'

Akmal turned to Layla. 'And your people?' He forgot to add Your Highness when he addressed her, but no one either cared or noticed. Layla was touched that in his darkest moment Akmal had thought of her subjects too. 'What will you tell them?'

'The truth—that I am still their Queen and my husband is now Prince Zafir of Calista. He chooses not to be King.'

'I told you, I am no Queen's consort…'

'As you wish…' Layla shrugged. 'You carry on with your princely ways… I will carry on with ruling Haydar—I wish you well.'

She had so much dignity and strength, and she would be fine, just fine, without him. Zafir knew that.

'Let us get this over with,' Layla said. 'I want to return to Haydar…'

'To be with your people…' Akmal nodded, but Layla shook her head and actually laughed.

'Actually, no! Of course that will happen, but I think I might just look after myself first—perhaps a small holiday is deserved. I would like some time with my sisters.'

As Akmal excused himself and left Layla

moved to do the same. She just could not stay strong for a moment longer, so she turned to go—but he caught her arm. There was one thing he needed to know.

'Are you pregnant?' Zafir asked. 'Is that why you need a holiday?'

'No to the first,' she said, 'and no to the second.'

If she carried on she would cry—and she had cried so much in the last few days that it would take a skilled make-up artist to prepare her for the cameras. 'I am going to listen to the press conference, and then I will prepare my speech…'

'I will come to Haydar soon…' He had demanded this separation, Zafir realised, yet now it was here he could not stand to see her go. 'In a couple of weeks—when you are—'

'That will not be necessary.'

'I promised you heirs…'

'And you will deliver.' It took every ounce of strength she could muster to step closer into his personal space, to let him breathe her scent again, to whisper in his ear and then afterwards look him in the eye. 'Think of me when you do it.'

He did not comprehend, so she explained

further. 'It's the twenty-first century Zafir—Haydar might not yet produce its own doctors, but it has marvellous hospitals…fertility centres.'

'No.'

'Yes,' Layla said. 'It is all or it is nothing.'

# CHAPTER EIGHTEEN

QUSAY was plunged into deep mourning.

The announcement had been made, and the press had been too stunned to ask many questions. Even the television newsreader, when they cut back to him, had struggled to continue for a moment. Even the maids who had brought Layla her lunch were weeping.

She was unable to stomach the palace any longer and, wanting to be close to the people, to gauge their reaction before she addressed her own, Layla put on her shawls and walked the sad streets. Women were wailing, grown men were crying, and there was a long queue forming outside the royal cemetery as the people lined up to pay their respects to Prince Xavian.

\* \* \*

There was no precedent.

The flood of advisors could not even agree as to how to announce Zafir, what name to use… Reams of paper lay shredded as they attempted to write his speech, but Zafir refused their final offering.

'I will speak without a script.'

'You have to say—'

'Who does?' he interrupted, with a pertinent point. 'Who has to say what? Am I their King? Am I Xavian today, or am I Zafir, addressing the people…?' He waited for an answer but of course there wasn't one.

But a deposed king apparently still had to look good, and he found himself sitting in a small room down the corridor from the main office as dressers and groomers fussed around him.

The dark shadows under his eyes were skilfully lightened, his jaw soaped ready for being shaved, and his hands were manicured… But he felt as if maggots were crawling over him, so he stood and shook them off.

Surely the people should see him as he was now—see his devastation, not a waxwork image of the King he once was?

Why did he have to look good as he broke their hearts? How could that possibly help? So he shooed them off and sat for a while in silence, trying to clear his mind. When he went into a bathroom, and washed the make-up from his face he stared at his unshaven jaw, at his red, bloodshot eyes.

He had lost everything.

Oh, he was still rich beyond his dreams.

Had gained a family, brothers, a less burdensome title.

And after this, the most difficult speech of his life, his real life—Zafir's life—would resume.

Yet he had lost her.

Kings did not cry—but he was no longer a king. And yet still he wouldn't go there—refused to give in to the blur before his eyes as he blindly pushed open a door and realised too late it was the wrong one. He heard her voice as she too lay back in the make-up chair and her advisors did what they always did: advised.

'Stress his knowledge...' a reedy voice said. 'Stress that though he is not a king, he is a Royal Prince of Calista—mention the wealth of his land and the rare pink diamonds, the rich bloodline your new offspring will bring to Haydar, say that this union is still good for our people…'

'I will speak my own words, Imran.'

'Your Highness…'

'You will leave me in peace to prepare my mind,' Layla snapped.

'But these are not ordinary times…'

'Then an extraordinary speech is called for!' Layla replied smartly, and Zafir felt just a hint of a smile on his lips as he heard that harsh, arrogant voice—just a tiny smile at the privilege of knowing her differently. 'Which I am more than capable of preparing if, for a little while at least, you would just leave me alone.'

And then it was just her and Baja, and Zafir knew he had to go, for his address to the people was soon. Gently he went to close the door—but then he heard her voice again.

Not the Layla he had met, not the Layla he had got to know, but a different Layla—one he did not recognise.

'I cannot do this, Baja….' He heard the terror in her voice, and the sheer weariness.

'You can, Your Highness…'

'I cannot face going out there. I am so tired, Baja…'

'Your people will be kind. They will…'

'I don't care about the people!' she sobbed, and Zafir felt his heart still at the raw honesty in her voice. 'Sometimes, Baja, sometimes, just for a little while, I actually want to care about *me*. Today it is not just about the King they have lost, or the arrangement that did not work, or the fact that they have to suffer still under the rule of a mere queen. It is about me too.'

'Layla…' Baja begged, dropping the title, wrapping her in her arms 'I know—I know more than anyone how hard this is for you…'

She was scared, Zafir realised, and his instinct was to soothe her—but it was no longer his place.

What was said next had him reeling.

'I do not want…' Layla wept.

'You must not say it,' Baja insisted.

'It is the truth. Tomorrow, next week maybe, I will be strong again, but for now I do not want to be Queen.'

'It will pass…' Baja implored. 'Remember that always this feeling passes. Some days you feel weak, and then you come back strong…'

'Not this time.'

'*Yes*, this time…' Baja insisted.

'I am tired of being strong…' Layla wept. 'Tired of always having to be strong. Tired of being hard. I am tired of being Queen…'

'You have no choice.' Baja took the make-up puff and dabbed at her cheeks. 'You have to be twice as strong as any man to rule Haydar.'

She did not.

Zafir knew that with him beside her she could be herself.

'Layla!' He watched her tense, watched her features snap back into place.

'What are you doing here? Surely it is time for your speech?'

'Your Highness!' The adviser's thin, reedy voice was back. 'I need to inform you—'

'Not now!' she barked at Imran, appalled as to what Zafir might have heard. She was struggling to keep control. 'I have told you I am busy. I have told you that I am to be left alone.'

'Of course…' Imran gave a small bow. 'Except there has been an earthquake in Haydar…'

Zafir watched her face pale.

'Are people hurt? How many are injured…?'

'We have only just got the news; there are no reports of injuries.'

'Where?' Layla asked. 'In the town or in the villages…?'

'It is early days yet…' the aide advised. 'I am sorry to trouble you at this difficult time…'

'Of course you had to inform me. Forgive my curt response.'

'One other thing…' He held out a folder. 'This document must be sent back to Haydar—the courier is waiting…'

'Of course…' Zafir's eyes narrowed as he watched her struggle for composure, her hand shaking as she signed her name.

'Do we know the size?' Zafir asked her aide. 'The size of the earthquake?'

'As soon as I have more information I will let you know.'

'Your Highness.' Suddenly a frantic Akmal appeared. 'What are you doing? It is time; the cameras are ready.'

Zafir was being guided through the palace corridors and led to a vast desk, and as he sat he pushed away the powder puff, pushed away his own thoughts, even pushed away Layla as for the last time he addressed the nation as their ruler. This had to be right. This wasn't about him. He had to be stronger than them, had to guide them through dark times, show them the way even when he was exhausted himself.

That was the lonely job of being King.

And Queen too…Xavian realised as the cameras rolled—Layla felt like this too.

'People of Qusay…' Zafir cleared his throat. 'I ask for your full attention. I ask that you listen to my words, that you halt your grieving long enough to hear what I say, and I pray that I calm your fears.' He glanced to Akmal, who stood as if on the edge of a cliff, abject terror on his face as his life's work crumbled. Even Akmal's wise eyes sought comfort, darting to Zafir's. Taking a deep breath, Zafir spoke not from a learned speech but from the very bottom of his soul—and delivered the most important speech in Qusay's history.

'Prince Xavian lies with his parents. Many of you have paid your respects today. The royal cemetery closed before sunset, but it will be open from sunrise to sunset for another week—we understand your need to honour Xavian, and perhaps to forgive the King and Queen, as I too am hoping to do.' He could see that Akmal's eyes were closed, as if in prayer. 'They tried to cheat death—that was their sin. But I am sure it was not their intention at the time to lie to their people. They were trying, I believe, not to cause this pain but to prevent it—impossibly, they wanted to keep their son, your future ruler, alive.

'I did not, could not understand, and yet I am starting to. Because the realisation has given me a choice... To cheat death again. To live the lie. To spare you this pain. But the people of Qusay are strong...' Zafir glanced to Akmal again, who opened his eyes and gave a slight nod. 'Strong, proud people, and they would prefer the pain of the truth—I know that. Lies spread—lies invade like a cancer. More people would have found out. My brothers who have mourned me knew the truth...my wife...'

Layla watched from another room, watched and wondered—because surely he *should* be King? Everyone was mesmerised listening to his assured, calming words.

'I would have lied to you...' He heard Akmal breathe in, knew that perhaps he had said the wrong thing, but pure truth was needed now. 'People of Qusay, if I had thought there was no other way I would have begged for my brothers' silence, I would never have told the Queen of Haydar, I would have taken this to my grave… But there is another path for you—the correct path—that should have been taken many years ago. King Yazan's sons, Kareef, Rafiq and Tahir, are your Princes. As I speak to you now, the elders are reaching out to them to inform them of the change… Prince Kareef of Qais will be your new King. He is, as you know, already a strong and fair ruler, and I trust you, the people of Qusay, to him.'

Pictures of Tahir, Rafiq and then Kareef flashed onto the screen. And Zafir walked out…stood in the corridor alone. Akmal came to him.

'Thank you.'

'Go back…' Zafir said. 'Tell me the response to the news…you have much work to do.'

And then he saw her—walking swiftly past, her face like porcelain, her eyes beautiful, her hair gleaming. She walked with confidence, her eyes dusting over his as she briefly nodded her head in greeting.

Calm, sophisticated, strong.

Yet Zafir knew different.

He watched her aides standing silently beside her, and then Zafir felt the weight of the jewel on his finger, felt the glow of the sapphire, and it alerted him in the same way his scars once had done. He watched as Imran gave a brief, almost imperceptible nod to one of the gathered journalists.

Zafir was wise, and he knew. After first checking one small fact, he asked Akmal to fetch Imran. The aide approached with a frown on his face, but it was nothing compared to the black smile that Zafir wore. Imran took a sharp intake of breath.

'Three point eight.' He watched as the aide looked puzzled. 'The earthquake you were so keen to inform the Queen about measured three point eight.'

'She likes to be kept informed.'

'My *shout* could do more damage than that.' Zafir's voice was dark and low, 'Let me see the document she signed.'

'That is Haydar business.' Imran's blink was rapid.

'Do you *want* me to shout?' Zafir offered.

'Do you *want* to find out the damage my shout can do?'

'Of course not,' the aide said quickly. 'But it is a private document. You are only Prince…'

'I am King,' Zafir said, and though it should have been said first to her, it felt good—it felt fantastic to say those words. 'I am King Zafir Al'Farisi of Haydar, and you would be foolish in the extreme not to hand me that document.'

The aide could hardly argue with that, and he stood and watched as Zafir read the paper-work—stood and gulped as slowly the new King shredded it. Then, without a word, Zafir walked across the room to Layla, who was seated at the desk—ready to face this alone, capable of facing this alone, and utterly prepared to do so.

Except she didn't have to.

'Bring me a chair so I can sit beside the Queen.'

He watched her eyes flash in annoyance. Here was not the place to argue, perhaps, but as he sat beside her Layla spoke in low tones.

'I would rather do this alone.'

'It will be easier for your people to hear the news with me beside you.'

'As you said in your speech, it is the time for more truth—not less. If I am to rule alone, save your occasional visit or your attendance at important functions. If you are to carry on with your princely ways...' She swallowed hard. 'I am requesting that you leave my side.'

'I cannot.'

She was about to summon aides, to get up and leave rather than sit through the charade of him loving her. There would be time for false unity later. Except something in his voice made her turn around—and, live to air, the Haydar people did not find their Queen gazing out at them from their TV screens, instead she faced her husband as he spoke.

'I would be proud and honoured to rule beside you—proud to help lead the people of Haydar.'

There was a pause—an agonising pause— as Layla realised they were live on air. Her pale cheeks flushed as she turned to the camera, words sticking in her throat.

'My subjects...' she started, and then faltered. The tears in her throat were too big to allow her to continue—but this was the most important speech in her country's history: there could be no tears, no weakness, no evidence of her emotions. And yet she couldn't speak. Then somehow, just as the silence had gone for too long, she managed to find the words to continue. Her voice, without waver, addressed the room, telling her people that all would be well, that Haydar would grow and prosper. Her muddled brain struggled to take in Zafir's declaration. She was too scared to believe, to trust that this time he meant it—that he wouldn't take it from her again.

'The Queen has agreed to questions.'

She had thought they would be about Zafir, about his role, but instead a journalist side-swiped her.

'You have agreed to postpone the building of the new teaching hospital?'

Layla could only blink, turning her face to her aides, who stared fixedly ahead.

'You signed the agreement this very day,' the journalist continued boldly—and Layla felt herself crumble, knew in that instant what had happened. Because it was what she had feared for so long. Her aides and advisors had waited for her moment of weakness and pounced, and there was nothing, *nothing* she could do. Years of work on behalf of her people had just been dashed by the stroke of her own pen.

'There is no agreement.' Zafir's strong voice filled the silent room.

'Zafir…' Her voice was strangled, her hand reaching for his to stop him, because she knew what she had done, but he took her fingers beneath the table and squeezed them firmly, and somehow in that moment a tentative trust emerged, and Layla knew that all she had to do was hold onto him.

'I have it from an impeccable source that the agreement has been signed,' the journalist challenged, then hastily added, 'Your Highness.'

'I suggest…' Zafir's voice held its own challenge '…you ask your source to produce the document—which he cannot, for it does not exist.'

Beneath the table his hand let go of hers, but she could still feel its warmth. It was more than a touch, it was support quietly offered when she felt that she couldn't go on, when it was all too much—it was how it could be.

On this, the saddest day, she glimpsed the possibility of wild dreams coming true.

'What will your role be?' Another journalist moved things along, asked the question that was on everyone's lips. 'Will you move between Calista and Haydar? Do you have any words for the Haydar people?'

'Today there is shock.' Zafir's voice was strong. 'In Qusay and Haydar, all the people are in shock—but tomorrow we will greet these changes. Qusay has a new King—King Kareef—and Haydar…'

He did the bravest thing, the most unexpected thing: Zafir gave a soft smile.

'As I said to my wife—she kissed a king and he turned into a prince… But a prince who is proud to serve you in whatever way is best. I will be proud to serve beside my wife as King.'

And all that was left to do was for Zafir to leave Qusay—to walk around the palace, to stare into the blue-eyed portraits of his predecessors and to finally understand why he had never felt as if he belonged.

'You will return…' Stefania assured him. 'Qusay will always welcome you…'

'I know that.'

'And you will come to Calista soon?' Zakari had tears in his eyes for the brother he had sought for so long. Now he had found him, he was leaving already.

'Of course,' Zafir said. 'I have brothers to meet, a life to catch up on—but there are other things to attend to now…' He looked over to Layla, who stood calm and poised, yet he knew that she trembled inside. 'We do not know the reaction in Haydar. It is unfair for Layla to return there alone.'

He hugged his brother and his sister-in-law, and then he kissed little Zafir, who had carried his memory. And, hard as it was to say goodbye, he knew it wouldn't be for long. No, the hardest part of leaving that night was saying goodbye to his trusted vizier—a man he had once considered smug, but who had stood by his side and had offered to continue to do so.

'You are needed here, Akmal,' Zafir said, 'to show King Kareef how things are done…' He took out the beautiful emerald necklace and handed it back to Akmal. 'For when the time is right…'

There was nothing else Qusay needed from him now, so he boarded the royal Haydar jet, took a seat by her side and stared out of the windows on take-off, watching the lights of Qusay grow dim and offering a prayer that the people would be safe under Kareef's leadership. He was grateful for Layla's quiet, yet he wished for the soft warmth of her hand.

Then Baja made her way over. 'Your Highness, the captain has asked me to apologise... I am so sorry...' Zafir frowned as the woman addressed her Queen, because Baja didn't look remotely sorry. 'There is a slight technical difficulty—we cannot broadcast the Haydar news in-flight.'

'How am I to gauge my people's reaction?' Layla snapped, then dismissed Baja, too weary to argue. But, even as she dismissed her, she wanted to call her back—because without Baja Layla was left alone with Zafir for the first time since the announcement, and she wasn't sure if she wanted to hear the answers to her questions. She didn't want to find out that it had been just a well-executed PR exercise—a slick speech to win her affection so that he might warm her bed tonight...

'I was confused...' He spoke first, and to hear such a commanding, assured man admit weakness had Layla turning her face to look at him. 'More confused than any man should ever be. I had nothing, Layla.'

'You have brothers, a kingdom to play in, polo…'

'Not my age,' Zafir countered, 'nor my name, not my staff, nor my title—and I wasn't even sure that I had a wife…'

'We stood before a judge.'

'That was not me.'

'It was you in bed that night…' Layla said. 'You, whatever your name or title is, who took so much more than my virginity. You showed me how it could be, and then, when the first sign of trouble came, you took it back.'

'I wanted to give you a choice,' Zafir said, and Layla realised it was the first time she had ever had a choice—oh, she had made plenty of decisions in her time, but a personal choice? There had been none—no question as to her life's journey. She had been groomed to be Queen, but even that would have been taken from her if a brother had come along. She had been expected to marry a man she had never met, to produce heirs, to rule Haydar—but never given a choice. And yes, in his own way, Zafir had offered her one.

'I am not what it said on the box…'

. He made her laugh, but it strangled in her throat and she started to cry.

'I do not need to check your signature. I do not need to read your speeches. I know you are now on my side. But I have lied to you, Zafir.' She gave a nervous swallow.

'I know…' he said. 'I heard you speaking with Baja of how sometimes it is too heavy a burden for you to carry…'

'Not that...' She shook her head 'I want not just your love, not just your body, but your wisdom too…' And he wrapped her in his arms and told her he knew. 'I am so weary of being strong, but it is not just that I have lied about…'

'Tell me.' He smiled, and she was no longer scared… Well, just a little bit.

'When we returned from the desert—' Layla gulped '—when you went to Calista, I lied to you.'

'I do not understand.'

"When you asked if I was with child…'

He was white now, but there was a hint of a smile waiting in the wings, and it urged her to go on. 'I lied when I said there was no baby…'

He kissed her, and it was wondrous, except he didn't quite understand.

'Why would you lie? You must have known that soon I would find out—and all that about fertility clinics…'

'I would never give away my title, but if I lost it…' She found it hard to explain. 'Or if that earthquake had been huge and I was returning tonight to face disaster—Zafir, I wanted you to be sure of what you were giving, and I wanted you to see all that you were giving up. It is all or nothing, and I wanted you to understand that. I can deal with anything if at night I can rest with you.'

'So now we have it all.'

The fear, the loneliness, that place he had inhabited for so many years, just flew from his chest and left his heart beating freely as her sweet words bathed his senses.

She was having his baby.

And as they absorbed the news he wasn't a king, nor a queen's consort, and Layla wasn't a queen. They were a couple instead—mortals who had made a miracle. The news was no longer about lineage and heirs—a new royal family was emerging that would rule with a new understanding of what really mattered in this world.

'I am nervous...' Layla admitted, gazing at the television screen. Kareef's face, as new ruler of Qusay, flashed before her eyes, then images of his brothers, Rafiq and Tahir, and images of the people in the street and their shocked reaction as they tried to take in all the changes. Her mind—as it had to even at the most tender of times—turned to her own people, and how *they* would accept the news. 'So much has changed.'

'So much has been put right,' Zafir countered, and the news report was turned off as the cabin lights were dimmed and they prepared for landing.

Layla could feel her heart hammering in her chest as she tried to gauge her people's reaction—she had left a robed virgin queen, left to merge Haydar with Qusay, promising to return with a king...

But as his hand wrapped around hers Layla knew, as she hoped her people would soon find out, that he was far better than the description on the box.

The people had their long-awaited King.

But perhaps it would take time for them to accept him.

'What are those lights…?' Zafir stared out of the window at the new land that awaited him.

'Probably the palace…' Layla said, not following his gaze, her eyes fixed ahead, for she truly hated landing.

'No along the streets…' Zafir started, but he didn't continue, feeling her tension and holding her hand as the wheels hit the tarmac and the plane slowly halted in a perfect landing.

The cabin lights came up, and Baja approached with a make-up assistant.

'Not now…' Layla shook her head. 'It's two a.m.….'

'There will be photographers…'

'Then shield me!' Layla said. 'I do not want photographs till I know my people's reaction—and,' she snapped as she stood, 'thanks to a *technical difficulty* I have been unable to watch the news. See that it is not repeated.'

But Baja wasn't listening, and instructed the make-up artist to continue, which she did, fussing with Layla's hair and dress even as she stood. Layla was too nervous to protest, too distracted to notice Baja's secret smile.

Zafir did, though.

The slight frown he directed to Baja showed a question, not annoyance, but she did not respond, just modestly lowered her eyes as still that smile danced on her lips.

And then the door opened, and Layla, quite simply, forgot to breathe.

The runway was within the royal grounds, yet shouts from the surrounding streets bridged the distance. The lights Zafir had seen were candles being held—surely every family in Haydar had come out to greet their royals?

'Cheer King Zafir of Haydar!'

'Cheer our loyal Queen Layla!'

'I wanted it to be a surprise…' Baja spoke out of turn. 'Your people love you, Layla, they only wanted to see you happy.' Wise dark eyes turned to Zafir. 'They love you too, Your Highness…'

It was dark, and it was late, but there was no question of going to bed.

Haydar wanted to celebrate—and the new royals obliged.

An open-top car was summoned, and they stood waving as they were driven through the cheering streets—never had Haydar been more vibrant.

This was the new beginning they had craved.

'I am home…' Zafir's words were lost in the deafening crowd, and Layla had to lean towards him to try and capture what he was saying, but it was too noisy for him to explain it.

For years, for endless long, lonely years, there had been a search for what he didn't know—for peace, happiness, for himself… And now here it was: freedom.

The freedom love brought; the freedom to be himself.

It was a freedom that couldn't be found in a palace he hadn't rightly inherited, and too much had changed for him to find true freedom in a land he had been torn from two decades ago.

'I am home,' he said again, and this time Layla heard him, and it didn't need clarification or explanation because she felt it too. Her people, her life, her responsibility—no longer a burden. Love was the ruler of this land now.

'I am home too,' Layla said. 'My home is with you.'

\* \* \* \* \*

*Harlequin Intrigue top author
Delores Fossen presents a brand-new
series of breathtaking romantic suspense!*
TEXAS MATERNITY: HOSTAGES
*The first installment available May 2010:
THE BABY'S GUARDIAN*

Shaw cursed and hooked his arm around Sabrina.

Despite the urgency that the deadly gunfire created, he tried to be careful with her, and he took the brunt of the fall when he pulled her to the ground. His shoulder hit hard, but he held on tight to his gun so that it wouldn't be jarred from his hand.

Shaw didn't stop there. He crawled over Sabrina, sheltering her pregnant belly with his body, and he came up ready to return fire.

This was obviously a situation he'd wanted to avoid at all cost. He didn't want his baby in the middle of a fight with these armed fugitives, but when they fired that shot, they'd left him no choice. Now, the trick was to get Sabrina safely out of there.

"Get down," someone on the SWAT team yelled from the roof of the adjacent building.

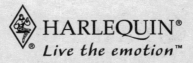

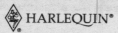

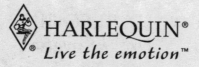

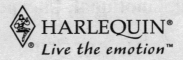

# HARLEQUIN®
## Super Romance®

## ...there's more to the story!

Superromance.
A *big* satisfying read about unforgettable characters. Each month we offer *six* very different stories that range from family drama to adventure and mystery, from highly emotional stories to romantic comedies—and much more! Stories about people you'll believe in and care about. Stories too compelling to put down....

Our authors are among today's *best* romance writers. You'll find familiar names and talented newcomers. Many of them are award winners—and you'll see why!

If you want the biggest and best in romance fiction, you'll get it from Superromance!

## Exciting, Emotional, Unexpected...

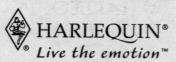

# HARLEQUIN®
## *Live the emotion*™

## Harlequin® Historical
### Historical Romantic Adventure!

*Imagine a time of chivalrous knights and unconventional ladies, roguish rakes and impetuous heiresses, rugged cowboys and spirited frontierswomen— these rich and vivid tales will capture your imagination!*

*Harlequin Historical... they're too good to miss!*

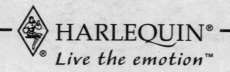